Train to Murder

Behavioral Unit Maine Series Book Two

Bella Lane

Blurbs

Content Warning

PLEASE READ CAREFULLY.

There are elements and themes within this book that some readers might find extremely upsetting. Please go to my website **www.be llalanebooks.com** under content warning for the list of potentially harmful topics. Please heed these as this book contains some heavy situations that some readers could find damaging.

Content

Prologue

UNKNOWN

Six weeks before

I walk up to the Amtrak train station located across from the Faren River in Largo, Maine. Looking at the building from the outside, it's white with glass windows all around. Its shape could have you thinking it's a stadium with a blue metal roof. I walk inside through the double doors that automatically open when you walk up to them and take in the spacious area. Looking up, there are more skylights in the roof, then there is a roof. I can see the night sky with a vast amount of stars shining down as it's still very early in the morning.

I look in front of me, and to the left is the ticket counter with a line of people already standing there to get their tickets for their destination. To the right of me, I can see the entrance to the restrooms. As I continue walking the length of the building, my footsteps muffled by the soft gray carpet on the floor, I see multiple seating areas with potted plants scattered all around.

On the right-hand side of the wall is a coffee bar and vending machines. I make my way to the coffee bar, needing the caffeine this early in the morning. Once I have my cup, I turn and take in my surroundings completely.

I'm amazed by the amount of people here so early in the morning. Some are dressed in pajamas, pulling their carry-on bag behind them as they make their way to the ticket line or to a seat. Others are dressed in business suits, carrying briefcases and laptop bags. Then there are some couples who aren't paying attention to anyone but each other.

I already purchased my ticket online, so with my coffee in hand, I take a seat in the waiting area near the doors that will lead out of the platform and continue looking around. I watch as a young blond girl walks in with a backpack strapped to her and steps into the ticket line.

This is the train to New York with a stop in Boston and will be leaving at four-thirty am. My eyes are on the couple currently making out, not caring that they are in public or that anyone may be watching them. Maybe they do know and don't care, though that's very foolish on their part. See, I know their secret, and it's one that will cost them everything.

I'm pulled from my prey, when I hear the call to board and see the double door to the platform open. Taking my time as I grab my bag, I watch everyone gather their things and head out to the platform.

I pull my ticket up on my phone, staying back but watching what is going on in front of me. No one notices me or even pays attention. I watch as people get in line by the car they are assigned. Most are in the line for business class, which makes sense, especially with how well they are dressed.

My ticket is for economy, and there is no seat number on it. I know the conductor will assign me a seat, so I am not worried. I continue looking over the people until my eyes land on the couple as they stand in the business line, two cars ahead of where I am currently standing in line.

My thoughts stray to wondering if they can feel they are being watched. Do they really care? From where I am standing, I would have to say no, they don't know nor care that they are being watched. They only have eyes and hands for each other at the moment.

I make my way in line to the conductor. "Ticket, please," he says.

I hand him my phone with the ticket on it, he scans it, then says, "Seat 21. Have a nice day."

I give him a little smile and step into the car, taking in the blue-backed fabric chairs. I walk down the aisle until I find my seat number. Thankfully, it's by the window and not the aisle.

I take a seat, keeping my bag on my lap, waiting for the train to start. I know there is a little over two hours before we pull into Boston for our first stop. As I sit on the train looking out the window, I see the people who are rushing to get on board before we leave the station.

My eyes drift to those around me that have already boarded, and like me, are sitting in their seats. They seem to take no notice of those around them. They are all either looking at their phones, pretending their life is too important to notice the people around them, or staring into the abyss, hoping no one notices them. I watch a couple of people close their eyes to catch some more sleep before they arrive at their destination.

I sit here wondering why they didn't opt for the private car, but I know why. The amount of money to get a private room on the train is insane, well insane for me, and judging by the pajamas they opted to wear, probably insane to them as well. I sit back in my seat, waiting for the train to start its journey. The young blond girl I had seen in the ticket line, hurries on board, taking the seat across the aisle from mine. She quickly takes her backpack off and places it in the seat next to hers, then sits in her seat, looking out her window.

I hear the conductor get on board and conduct his checks as he walks down the aisle, then he says, "We will be leaving the station shortly, folks."

No one says anything as they continue to settle into their seats. I turn to look at the young blond girl again. She looks to be seventeen, maybe eighteen, and I can feel the excitement buzzing off her, but also nervousness. Makes me wonder what she is doing and where she is going, but I refuse to ask. Conversations are best left to other people.

The train starts to pull away from the station, so I lean my head back and close my eyes until we get up to speed. Once the train is at full speed, the conductor comes through and says, "The cafe is open for anyone needing anything." He then continues walking to the next car, presumably to tell them the same thing.

I place my bag under the seat in front of me, and just as I scoot to the aisle to get up, the young blond whispers, "Excuse me."

I look up at her, and she gives me a shy smile before continuing on. "I apologize for bothering you, but I've never been on a train before, can you tell me how to get to the café?"

I mull over her words and then before I even think about what I'm saying, I tell her, "You can follow me."

"Oh, thank you so much. I promise not to be a bother," she says quietly but with a bright smile.

I'm not sure why I allowed myself to speak to her, but I shrug like it's no big deal. As we walk down the aisle, I point out the bathroom to her before we leave our car and head into the next one. I can hear her breathing behind me, as I look the people over while I continue to walk down the aisle. Some are on their laptops working, some are on their phones typing. I pass a few who have their eyes closed, sleeping.

The couple that was making out at the station is sitting in the back of the second car we go through, the man is touching all over the woman as she giggles. The man is next to the aisle, and the woman is by the window. There is only an empty row behind them and no one around them for five rows. I continue making my way to the cafe, needing as much caffeine as I can get.

The young girl continues to follow me to the cafe. As we stand in line, I can hear her mumbling to herself.

I turn to look at her, unable to help myself, and ask, "Are you okay?"

"Yeah. I'm just a bit nervous, having never been on a train before. It's just a little weird feeling the train move as I'm standing," she says.

Though I know I shouldn't, I ask, "Where are you headed?"

"I'm going to New York to visit NYU," she says with that bright smile, then I watch it falter.

"Why do you seem unhappy about that?" I ask.

"I am happy, but I'm also worried about what my parents will think when they find out," she says with a sigh.

"How old are you?" I ask, curious to know if I was right when I first glanced at her.

"Seventeen," she responds.

"Did you not tell them?"

"No. My mom doesn't want me going to college far from home, and to her, New York is far from home."

I can see the sadness in her eyes as she speaks about her mom being disappointed.

"Are you from Maine?"

"Yes," she replies with a deep sigh.

"So why are you going?" I ask her as we continue standing in the line, waiting for the other patrons to get their orders.

"I just want to visit the campus and see if it's as exciting as I think it is. I'll be starting my senior year of high school in the fall, and I plan to do the other college tours with my parents around Maine, but I know they would never agree to do a tour at NYU. A few of my friends plan on attending NYU, and I need to know if it's a place where I could fit in."

I nod my head in understanding. "Well," and I pause, not knowing her name.

"Rayeanne," she says, smiling again.

"Well, Rayeanne, I would suggest after the visit, you come clean to your parents immediately. Do they even know where you are right now?"

She shakes her head before saying, "They think I'm with my travel soccer team, and as long as I get back home later tonight, they will never know I did this."

"If you find this is the University you want to attend, you should tell them, and then maybe plan a trip as a family together so they can understand why you want to go there," I tell her.

"Maybe," she mumbles, now looking deep in thought.

I turn back around in time to see I am next, and I place my coffee order, I also grab the girl's hot chocolate, then we make our way back to our designated car, passing the couple not paying attention to anyone around them. I take note of the pale white circle on his ring finger where a ring should be.

I continue leading Rayeanne and myself back to our car and seats. For the next hour, we continue talking about her ambitions and goals for her future.

"Have you decided what you plan to major in?" I ask, deeply curious now.

"I want to study law and become a lawyer. My grandfather is a detective where we live, and I'd like to follow in his footsteps, but I don't want to be a cop," she says with excitement in her eyes.

"How do your parents feel about that?"

"They love the idea. To them it's one of the safest and best jobs on the planet," she tells me, wrinkling her nose up.

I can't help the laugh that escapes me.

After a little while longer of conversation, Rayeanne finally closes her eyes, not being able to keep them open any longer. I sit back in my seat, knowing it won't be much longer before we will be arriving in Boston. I know I still have something that I need to do before I debark.

When we have about fifteen minutes left of the trip. I look over and see Rayeanne is still asleep. I get up from my seat, carrying my bag with me, and make my way through the second car where I stop at the bathroom, pull out a black sweatshirt, and throw it over my top.

I leave the bathroom, making my way to the third car. I watch the conductor as he exits the car, going the opposite way from where I came. Probably going to the cafe car to get him a snack before we stop. I slide into the row behind the make-out couple, they both look to have their eyes closed, but still holding hands.

How poetic, I think to myself.

I pull my gloves on and slip the needle out of my bag. Taking the cap off, I reach around to the man's arm as it sits on the armrest, sticking him quickly as I release the liquid into his arm. I watched as his arm jerked, but then stilled. I pull out my knife, looking at my watch, waiting for the right moment. I can feel the train start to slow down, and I quickly grab the female's dark hair, pulling her head back, and before she can utter a noise, I slice across her neck.

I watch as the blood spurts onto the back of the seat in front of her. I look over and see the male has his eyes open, watching what I did. I know he wants to do something, but unfortunately, he can't. I grab his ring finger, where the pale white circle shines like a beacon, and I cut his finger off. I lean his head back and slice across his neck, watching the blood spurt across the back of the seat in front of him, just like the female.

I hear a gasp behind me and turn to see Rayeanne standing there, in utter horror and shock having seen what I just did. I quickly grab her, holding the knife to her throat, and whisper in her ear, "I really wish you hadn't seen that. Don't utter a sound, do you understand me?"

She nods her head. I look at my watch and see we still have a few minutes until we pull into the Boston station. I lead her out of the car, into the next, and straight into the bathroom.

"We don't have much time," I say as I pull my gloves off, stick them into the zip lock bag I brought, then pull off my black sweatshirt. I pull out another sweatshirt, handing it to Rayeanne.

"Put this on," I tell her as I fix my clothes.

I watch as she quickly does what I tell her, then I grab her hair, wrapping it up, and place a ball cap on her head. Once we are done, I grab my bag and lead her to the door where we will be exiting. I put the knife to her side, while I stand behind her, waiting for the doors to open so we can exit the train.

"You don't have to do this. I promise not to tell anyone," she pleads in a whisper.

"I wish I could believe you, Rayeanne, but see, you already told me your grandfather is in law enforcement, and you want to be a lawyer. I don't think your conscience will allow you to keep this to yourself."

"What are you going to do to me?"

"I don't know yet," I answer her honestly.

I know I should kill her, but she's so young. I knew I should never have started a conversation with her.

"What about my bag?" she asks quietly.

"It will go to the lost and found. Give me your phone," I whisper in her ear, knowing she like any teenager, has it on her. She whimpers as she pulls it out of her pocket and hands it to me.

I turn it off, and as soon as the doors open, I drop it between the platform and the train.

"Walk, keep your head down, and don't cause a scene, or I will stab you with no chance for survival, do you understand?"

"Yes," she whispers, keeping her head down as I told her, she walks in the direction I am pushing her in.

Soon, I'll have to decide what to do, but for now, she'll have to come with me.

Chapter One

MYA

Present Day

I'm just getting out of the shower when my phone rings. I walk over to it and see Declan's name.

"Declan, what's going on?" I ask as I answer the phone.

"Eric wants everyone at the office, Kim is missing," he says, sounding distraught.

"What do you mean Kim is missing?" I ask Declan, but he hangs up the phone.

I quickly pull some clothes on, pull my long-wet hair into a messy bun, grab my keys, and head to the office.

When I get there, I see Eric holding Michelle upright.

"Eric, what is going on? Declan said Kim is missing?" I ask him.

"Let's wait for everyone to get here, and I will explain," Eric says as he looks down at Michelle.

I look at Michelle, she is absolutely pale, but trying her hardest to be strong. Kim is Michelle's best friend, and they have been since college. If anyone would know where Kim would be, it's Michelle, and if she doesn't know, then this is serious.

Looking at Eric and Michelle, I still can't believe they got married in secret, and none of us knew. Well, we suspected they were in a relationship, but marriage never crossed our minds, however looking at these two together, you can see they are a perfect fit. They are both each other's weaknesses and strengths.

I internally sigh wondering if I'll ever get lucky enough to find my other half, then I shake my thoughts away as this is not the time to be worrying about myself or lack of a love life.

Heath comes running into the conference room wearing only a pair of sweatpants and a t-shirt. The look on his face screams worry for his friend. Declan is right behind Heath, and before Heath can open his mouth, Eric says, "Wait until everyone is here."

Heath nods and takes a seat next to me, but I can feel anxiousness rolling off him.

Declan immediately takes a seat at the table, looking lost, and I have to wonder if there is more going on with him and Kim than just being friends. I know they have been spending some time together lately, as Kim is Michelle's maid of honor and Declan is to be Eric's best man when Eric and Michelle redo their wedding in two months. Would I be surprised if they took a page out of Michelle and Eric's book and are doing the secret romance? No, but again I could be reading more into their relationship than what actually is.

After another ten minutes, Frankie finally comes in looking sweaty and disheveled.

"Sorry, boss, I was on my way back from the gym when I received the call," he says.

"Now that everyone is here," Eric begins as Frankie takes a seat. "We have determined that Kim is missing."

"Why do we think she is missing?" I ask, needing more than what is being said.

Eric, understanding what I'm asking, says, "Declan went by her place to pick her up and found her vehicle in the driveway, her wallet, and keys in the house, but she was not there. When he tried to call her, it went straight to voicemail. I also tried to ping her location and found her phone to be off. After calling Heath and Frankie, we realized no one had seen or heard from her since she left the park."

The fact that her phone is off is worrisome, Kim never turns her phone off. Her car, wallet, and keys being at her house isn't that strange as Kim likes to walk to the shops around her area.

"Did anyone check the shops in her area?" I ask as I think it.

"Yes, I went by every single one, and no one has seen her today," Declan says in a low whisper.

I look over at Heath and can see the tracks of the tears as they coat his face. Declan looks completely lost, and Frankie looks stunned.

"What do you need us to do, Boss?" I ask since it seems everyone else forgot we are agents.

"We need to search her property for any clues that may tell us what happened to her," Eric says. "We treat this like any other crime scene. Right now, we are looking at the fact that it's only been just over two hours since she was last seen. I know we are jumping in early, but this is one of our own, and we need to find her," he says, looking down at his wife.

"I will send a data request to public safety for the Uber and Lyft data, and then I will call all the taxis, airports, and the train station to ensure she didn't have an emergency that caused her to leave without notice," I say as I grab a laptop and begin filling out the required form before searching for taxi companies.

"That's good. Declan, you and Heath go to her house and search it for anything you may have missed while you were there," Eric tells them.

"I'll call her mom and make sure there was no family emergency that would have called her away," Michelle says, pulling out her phone as she walks out of the conference room.

"Why were you at her house to begin with?" Frankie asks Declan.

"What the hell does that matter? If he hadn't been there, we wouldn't know she was missing until much later. You really need to get your priorities straight," Heath barks at Frankie.

"We had plans for dinner to go over some of the wedding details for Eric and Michelle," Declan says before walking out of the conference room with Heath as he shakes his head.

I look over at Frankie and see his face is red, from anger or embarrassment, I'm not sure, and unfortunately, I don't have time to decipher it, since there are twenty cab companies alone in Largo, and I begin making calls.

"What do you need me to do, Boss?" I hear Frankie ask.

"I need you to pull her phone records for the last three months. Let's see if there is anything unusual in them that could help us. "

"On it."

Frankie walks out of the conference room just as the dispatcher for the first taxi company on the list answers the phone.

"Largo Taxi Company, how can I help you this evening?"

"Hi, this is Agent Mya Morgan with the FBI. I'm looking to see if any of your cabs picked up a passenger tonight, by the name of Kimberly Santiago, from address, 2121 Sands Dr, in Largo?"

"Let me check the call records, one moment, please, Agent."

She places the call on hold, and all I hear is the elevator music for what seems like an eternity but was probably less than two minutes.

"Sorry for the wait, Agent, no, we had no callouts or pick-ups for that location."

"Thank you. Have a good evening," I tell her before hanging up.

I quickly cross that one off my list and dial the next.

Two hours later, I hang up the phone to the last taxi company. I rub my eyes, as Eric and Michelle look over at me. "Not one taxi in Largo picked up Kim," I tell them, and watch Michelle's shoulders sag in defeat.

"I talked to her mom, and there is no emergency at home," she admits.

Heath and Declan walk into the conference room, with Frankie following behind them.

"Boss, we searched her whole house, we can't see anything missing. Her go bag is still packed and on the floor of her closet, as well as her suitcase," Heath says.

"Kim didn't leave on her own," Declan says angrily.

"Boss, I was able to get her phone records after some back and forth with the provider," Frankie begins, looking down at the sheet. "Seems, there were some calls from an unknown number, and when I ran it, it came back to a burner phone."

"A burner phone?" Eric asks, sounding confused as the rest of us look.

"Yes, Sir. Seems the number started calling her three months ago. It looks like she only answered it twice in the beginning, but then quit answering it," Heath says, looking at the phone log before handing it to Eric.

"I recall a couple of times being with her and her phone would ring, she would look at it, then ignore it," Michelle says with a look on her face that she was thinking back to those times.

This is the first time I'm hearing about phone calls, and I try to think back to when she and I were together, and for the life of me, I can't remember her phone ever ringing where she didn't answer it.

"Anything on your end?" Heath asks me, but I can only shake my head no.

"I still have the train station and airport to call, plus I'm still waiting to get the reports from Uber and Lyft, but I can tell you for certain no taxi company picked her up," I tell him, as I search for the airport number next.

"Frankie, see if you can trace that burner phone back to where it was purchased. It's a long shot to think the place may still have video, but it's our only lead right now," Eric says.

"On it, Boss."

"Declan, Heath, I need you two to look into any of our past cases and see if anyone has been paroled or bent on revenge. I need to know if this is about Kim only, or is the whole team in danger?" Eric says.

"That's a lot of people, but we are on it, Boss," Heath says.

"You think this could be someone out for revenge?" Michelle asks Eric.

"I don't know, to be honest, but we must look at every possibility. Is there anyone in Kim's personal life that would want to harm her?" he asks Michelle.

"Not anyone I know of. She didn't hang around a lot of people outside of work or me, but I don't know much about her relationship with her neighbors," Michelle admits, chewing on her lip.

"I'll look into her neighbors, why don't you go home and get some rest. I'll call you if we learn anything," Eric tells her.

"I'm okay. I need to be here, Eric, not at home."

"Okay, then you can help me," he says, leading her out of the conference room.

I pick up the phone and begin calling the airlines.

Chapter Two

SHANE

Boston

The ringing of the phone pulls me out of my semi-slumber, and I swear I just laid down in the bed and closed my eyes. I look over and see it's seven am. "How is it possible to sleep for five hours and yet feel like you haven't slept at all," I groan to myself as I roll over and pull the phone from the nightstand, hitting the answer button.

"Detective Maguire," I answer gruffly.

"Sorry to wake you, Shane, but we have another one," my partner, Detective Nora Riley says, and I sigh.

"Where?"

"At the south side train station," she conveys.

"A couple?" I ask.

"Yeah."

"Did you call the coroner?"

"Of course. He's currently on his way."

"Good. I'm on my way as well," I tell her, hanging up as I roll out of bed.

This makes three couples in six weeks killed on a train.

I make my way into the bathroom to get ready. As I brush my teeth, I take in the dark circles around my eyes from the lack of sleep. The homicide rate in Boston seems to have shot up since the new year started, and we are only five months into it.

I shake my head as I try to see the blue in my eyes, but they are overtaken by the red from being bloodshot. I need sleep, but sleep is a luxury I can't afford.

Unfortunately, there aren't many homicide detectives on the force anymore, and those of us that are still here are stretched thin. With budget cuts the way they are, our division has suffered across the board in the state. We no longer have an overtime budget like we once had, and we are unable to hire new detectives, so basically, we continue doing our job for the people without benefits, sleep being one of them. Everyone is burned out, and if it wasn't for the fact that I love what I do, I would probably hang it up just like the others have.

I notice I have two-day-old stubble on my face, so I grab my shaving cream and razor and do a quick shave. I don't have the luxury of taking my time. I need to get to the scene when the coroner gets there.

I finish shaving and wipe my face with the towel. Walking out of the bathroom, I walk into my closet, grabbing the first pair of black slacks and a white shirt that I see. I quickly pull them on, then grab a tie. Making quick work, I pull on black socks and slide my black oxfords on.

Walking back into the bathroom, I grab a comb and quickly run it through my not quite long, but not quite short hair.

Walking back into my closet, I grab a black suit jacket and put it on. When I step in front of the mirror, I look like the ever forty-year-old professional with bloodshot eyes, that I am.

I go back into the bathroom, grab my Visine, and quickly drop two drops in each eye. That will have to do. I make my way to the front door grab my wallet and keys out of the bowl that's on the console table. Getting in my car, I head to the train station to begin, what I know is going to be another long day.

I pull up to the South Station, parking my car at the curb. The South Station has a curved facade on the outside with an eagle-topped clock. It's made of steel, concrete, and glass. I walk inside, massive windows everywhere except on the roof. There are a total of twenty-seven ticket booths around the facility, as well as a grand waiting room. The floor is made of a marble mosaic pattern, and the walls are fashioned from granite, enameled brick, and plaster.

There is an elevator located down the corridor from the main information booth, and it's perfect for getting to the Red Line platform if you don't want to take the stairs and escalator. The Silver Line goes to Logan Airport or Seaport.

I see the Amtrak lounge just past the information booth on the left. For travelers, there is complimentary coffee and newspapers.

There are twenty different places to eat from in the train terminal, as well as six retail businesses for shopping things you may need or have forgotten. There are currently three ATMs throughout the facility. I look up and see the big board with departing and arrival information, all the destinations in orange, and the times are in green.

Before I find what I am looking for, Officer Buckley finds me.

"Detective Maguire, Detective Riley is waiting for you this way," he tells me before turning off and leading me to the platform.

"Is the coroner here?" I ask him quietly so as not to alert any of the passengers.

"Yes, Sir. He just got here and is currently viewing the scene."

I nod, though he can't see me. I continue following him. Once we are on the platform, I pull my gloves out and put them on. Officer Buckley takes me to a Business Class car.

I walk on, seeing the coroner in the back, looking over the bodies of the male and female sitting together. Detective Riley turns and looks at me, giving me a nod. I notice her blond hair is neatly in a bun and pinned to the top of her head. Her suit is hanging off her, showcasing the amount of weight she has lost over the last six months. She looks older than her thirty-eight years, and her brown eyes look as sleep-deprived as I feel.

I take in her demeanor, knowing these cases are hard on her given the fact that her own husband was murdered on a train six months ago in a robbery gone wrong. He was stabbed multiple times. Her best friend Courtney White, who was also her husband's secretary, was with him that day and seemed to have disappeared.

I know she hasn't slept much in the past six months, spending her free time searching for Courtney and trying to find the person responsible for killing her husband. There were no witnesses, and the consensus is he must have been protecting his secretary from a possible gang to have been stabbed that many times.

She stands rigid, watching the coroner look over the couple. The Commander has tried to get her to take some time off to process her loss, but she insists that working is the only way she can function.

I slide into the seats two rows from where the coroner is currently working from. I look over at Nora, "Where did this train come from?"

"Maine," she tells me quietly.

"Just like the other two," I mutter more to myself, but I catch her nodding.

"Who found the couple? The conductor?" I ask.

"No, this time it was another passenger, Ms. Lauren Harper. She was heading to the exit back here when she spotted them. At first, she thought they were asleep, then she noticed the blood," she relays to me in a formal tone.

The coroner, Maxwell McBride, but everyone calls him Max, steps back and looks over at me.

"Just like the other two male victims, his ring finger has been cut off. Both victims have their throats cut, one clean slice, no hesitation," he tells us.

"So, you think the same person is responsible?" I ask him, needing confirmation.

"Definitely."

I rub my face with my hand, feeling some stubble that I missed during my quick shave this morning. I look over at Nora and say, "We are going to need to call the FBI."

"Yeah, I was thinking the same thing," she says with a sigh.

We both hate involving other agencies in our investigations, especially the FBI, but I can't see any way around it. Whomever this person is, they are boarding in Maine and getting off here in Boston.

The better question besides why are they doing this is are they from here or Maine? If they are from Maine, how are they getting back to Maine? Another train? A car? A bus? More questions, and very few answers.

"Here, I found this in his pocket," he says, passing me the man's wallet and cell phone. I open the wallet to find the victim's driver's license with his name and home address.

Max passes Nora the woman's purse.

"Did you get pictures?" I ask Nora as I pass her the victim's wallet to place in an evidence bag.

"Yes, I did, and so did the crime scene techs before Max got here."

"Good. Max, they are all yours. Let me know if you find out anything else. I need to make some calls," I say before I debark off the train, with Nora following close behind me.

"I'm going to stop by the security room to see about getting copies of the video footage of the train's arrival as well as passengers who departed the train," I tell her, wishing Amtrak would get cameras for all their cars and not just in the operator's space. That would make catching a killer easy, but nothing in this world is ever easy.

"I'll head back to the station, log in the evidence we have so far, and begin the paperwork. I'll also get the photos printed and have them ready by the time you get back. We can put them against the others and see if anything is different," she tells me, looking beat.

"When was the last time you slept?" I ask her.

"I sleep. I got a couple of hours last night," she tells me defensively. I give her a hard look, and she sighs.

"Look, I won't lie, it's hard to sleep without Ben beside me, but even worse, not knowing where Courtney is. Every time I close my eyes, I see Ben's body, and then I begin to wonder if Courtney is alive, what is she going through? It's almost like someone is taunting me with these bodies," she says, waving her hand toward the train. "The last two men were businessmen, and the women were their personal assistants doing their jobs, this couple will probably end up being the same," she says.

"I get it, and you are probably right," I say with my own sigh, as it does feel like someone could be taunting Nora. "Listen, go back to the station, and I'll meet you there. We can call the FBI, bring them up to speed, and see how they want to handle it," I tell her.

"Okay," she says softly, grabbing all the evidence bags and placing them in a box.

"Officer Buckley, please help Detective Riley get these to her car, I need to go to the Security room," I tell the officer, and he nods.

Once I have the videos from this morning, I walk over to Starbucks in the station and order a venti. I need the caffeine if I'm going to stay awake. Once I have the coffee, I leave the train station and drive to the precinct.

I can't help but rub my eyes and forehead, knowing I need to make a call. Though a part of me would love to have the FBI come in and take over the case so I can focus on other homicide cases, the other part of me, the part that is a Detective through and through, doesn't want anyone coming in and taking my case from me.

I let out a sigh, park the car, grab my coffee, and head inside. I just know today is going to be a long day.

I walk into the station, and Commander William Doyle is waiting for me. "Maguire, you and Riley, in my office now," he calls out.

I don't bother stopping at my desk but continue walking until I'm standing in the Commander's office. The walls are gray, with one small window made of bulletproof glass, making it difficult to see out of. The Commander's gray metal desk is messy with paperwork, a computer, and his phone.

He directs us to sit in the old, worn-out chairs that are in need of repair or replacement across from his desk, if we had a budget to do it.

Nora and I take a seat in the chairs, as I look over the Commander. His face is matching the red in his hair, and I'm not sure what has him agitated so early in the morning.

"Is it true?" he asks.

"Is what true, Sir?" I ask, utterly confused.

"Is it true there was another two bodies found on a train this morning?" he asks.

"Yes, Sir. We just came from the scene," Nora responds as I take a drink of my coffee.

"Did this train arrive from Maine as well?"

"It did," I say.

"Are we sure these murders are like the other two?"

"Yes, Sir. The coroner already confirmed the details are the same," Nora says quietly.

"Are you sure you want to stay on this case, Riley?" he asks with a softness in his voice.

"Yes, Sir. These families deserve justice," she responds.

"Well, you know what this means, don't you?" he inquires, looking at both of us.

"Yes, Sir. We are going to have to call the FBI," I tell him.

"Exactly, and we are going to have a bunch of suits wanting to take over our department," he says, anger returning to his voice.

"I won't lie, Commander, as much as I don't want to involve them, they do have better technology than we do," I say, trying to find a positive in the situation we currently find ourselves in.

"Six deaths that literally roll into our city," he says, shaking his head before picking up the phone.

I look over at Nora and she shrugs her shoulders, but we turn back and watch the Commander as he waits for whomever he is calling to pick up on the other end.

"Agent Anderson, it's Commander Doyle from Homicide Division. How are you today?"

"Good. Listen, we have an issue. You have time for a meeting?"

Nora and I can't hear the other side of the conversation, so we sit here listening to the Commander talk as he sets up the meeting.

"You can come here, or we can go to you."

"My two Detectives and myself."

"Shane Maguire and Nora Riley."

"Yeah, that's right."

"Thirty minutes? Yeah, that's fine. We will be waiting for you," he responds before hanging up the phone and looking at us.

"We may as well rip this band-aid off now. He will be here in thirty minutes, I suggest you pull all your files together and meet us in the conference room," he tells us as the phone rings again, and we are dismissed.

Nora and I walk out of his office and straight to our desks to gather up the files, pictures, and reports needed to discuss this with the FBI Agent. Once we have everything, we make our way into the conference room to wait for the Agent and the Commander, while we lay everything out that we currently have.

I still need to look up the next of kin for our latest victim and make the notifications that their loved ones are no longer with us, while also finding out everything I can about why they were on that train or if they have any enemies that would want to harm them?

I get pulled from my thoughts when I hear the Commander say, "They are waiting for us in here."

Commander Doyle waves his hand to allow the Agent to step into the conference room first. Looking at him, he looks to be maybe in his forties, with dark hair and gray at the temples. His eyes are dark brown with an intense seriousness in them. He is currently wearing a black suit, a white shirt, and a black tie. I would equate his attire to what they wear in the Men In Black movies.

"Agent Anderson, this is Detective Maguire and Detective Riley," Commander Doyle introduces us before they take a seat in the chairs at the table.

"Why am I here?" Agent Anderson asks.

I look at Commander Doyle, and he nods, so I begin. "Sir, in six weeks, we have had six deaths on the Amtrak train coming in from Maine."

"Wait, are you telling me there has been a murder a week, and you are just now informing us?" Agent Anderson interrupts me.

I take a deep breath to control my emotions before continuing, "No, Sir. What we have is three couples, one male and one female killed on a train. This morning was the third couple. The last two were found to be a male boss and his assistant. We are pretty sure the couple found this morning will be the same type."

I pass him over the first two files, and Nora passes him the pictures that were taken at the crime scene.

"Where did you say this train came from?" he asks.

"It originated in Maine, Sir," I tell him.

"I see. Do you believe this is the work of a serial killer?" he inquires, looking at me.

"Unfortunately, I don't see how it is not," I reply.

"What about you, Detective Riley? Are you able to work this case, given the circumstances so similar to your own experience?" he asks her.

I shouldn't be surprised that he pulled our background.

"Sir, with all due respect, these murders are nothing like my husband's death or my best friend missing."

"Hmmm," he hums before saying, "I know just a team who specialize in these situations. I will give Agent Chandler a call. I will need a copy of these files to send to him."

"Let me go make you a copy," Nora says, leaving the room.

Five minutes later, she comes back with a thumb drive and hands it over to Agent Anderson. "Here you go, Sir."

Agent Anderson stands, taking the thumb drive, and says, "Thank you. The team will be in touch with you shortly."

He walks out of the room, and I look over at Commander Doyle. He looks back and shrugs without saying a word, before walking out of the conference room.

Nora looks at me and says, "Well this should be fun."

"Agree, but first, we need to find next of kin for our two victims and make notifications," I tell her as we both walk out of the conference room.

Chapter Three

MYA

I click end on my last phone call to the train station, crossing it off my list. There are no tickets anywhere that were purchased in Kim's name. I'm still waiting on Uber and Lyft data, but so far, everywhere else points to her not leaving on her own. I check my phone and see it's just after one am. It's been seven hours since Kim was last seen. I can't help but rub my tired burning eyes.

Frankie is chasing the burner phone, but I don't know if he is going to have any luck with the amount of time that has passed. Declan and Heath are currently going through the files of all our cases over the years, and they look exhausted.

Eric walks into the conference room looking over at me, and I can only shake my head. I watch his subtle nod as he looks down the table at Heath and Declan. Michelle comes to stand next to him looking tired and defeated.

"I want everyone to go home and get some rest, we will meet back here at seven am," Eric says, and before anyone can protest, he adds, "I know you all want to find Kim, I do too, but we are no good to her if we work ourselves to exhaustion and miss something crucial that could save her sooner. Go home, get a couple of hours of sleep, and come back ready to dive into finding her. Maybe once we all have some sleep, someone might think of something we haven't already thought about."

He looks down at Michelle, pulling her into his side, and wraps his arm around her. "Let's go," he says, walking out of the conference room.

We all begrudgingly get up and follow him out of the conference room, knowing he is right. We won't be any good to Kim if we don't take care of ourselves. We need to treat her like any other case we work.

We all make our way out of the office and watch as Eric closes and locks the door. Heath pushes the elevator button, and when the doors open, we all pile in, making our way down to the lobby.

Once in the parking lot, everyone makes their way to their respective vehicles.

"I want everyone to be careful going home, once you get there, check-in using the group chat, so I know everyone made it home safely, and I will see you all back here at seven am," Eric tells us before opening the passenger door to allow Michelle into the car.

I get in mine, start it up, and watch as Frankie, Heath, and Declan pull away before I follow behind, with Eric following me.

Though the streets of Largo are empty and quiet, it takes me a little longer than normal to get home. My eyes are blurry and burning and I know it's because I'm tired. I can hear the chimes of the texts going off, letting me know that everyone is starting to get home.

I pull into my apartment complex and breathe a sigh of relief that I am finally here. What should have only taken ten minutes, took me twenty tonight. I quickly grab my stuff, knowing if I sit here too long, I'll fall asleep in the car, so I get out, and make my way up the stairs and to my door. Once inside, I lock the door and pull out my phone, looking at the chat to see I'm the last one to check in, so I quickly send off a text.

Made it home.

Eric responds,

See everyone at seven. Get some sleep.

I trudge my way to the bedroom, and without even undressing, curl up on the bed. I don't remember shutting my eyes, but my alarm clock wakes me at six. I turn it off, wishing I could just close my eyes and go back to sleep, but then I instantly remember Kim is missing. It's enough to jolt me out of bed.

I quickly make my way to the kitchen to start a pot of coffee before jumping into the shower. I don't have the luxury of time to enjoy the shower, so I quickly wash up, get out, wrap a towel around my hair and another around my body, and then brush my teeth before going to the kitchen to get me a cup of coffee.

I grab a cup out of the cabinet above the coffee pot and pour what I consider to be liquid gold, into my cup. I add a little sugar and creamer, stirring before I take the first sip.

"Mmmm," I moan as the hot liquid goes down my throat.

I take my cup back to the bedroom with me as I only have twenty minutes before I need to leave to make it to the office at seven, and I need to get dressed. I place the cup on the bathroom counter. I take the towel off from around my body, placing it in the hamper. I make my way to my dresser, pull out my matching bra and underwear set, as well as pantyhose and put them on.

I go back into the bathroom, take the towel off my head and toss it in the hamper as well. I grab my comb and begin combing my long brown hair until it's smooth. I proceed to French-braid it, so I can pin it up.

People have often commented to me how they wish they could French braid their own hair, but their fingers get confused, and they mess up. I'm often asked how I'm able to do my own hair, and it still looks so professional. I learned early on how to do my own hair, but where most people can do someone else's hair, I can only do mine.

To be honest, I've been doing things myself since I was a kid. I don't even think twice about it. Both my parents worked while I was growing up, so they would ensure I was awake to get ready for school before they walked out the door. Sometimes mom would have breakfast made for me, but most of the time I was left to take care of myself as there was no one else around to do it for me. It was the same when I got home from school. My parents worked twelve hours a day, so by the time they came home, I already had homework completed and dinner ready for them.

It's probably one of the reasons I have a hard time dating and have never been married. I'm thirty-five years old, and I'm so used to doing things for myself that it's hard to allow someone else to do things for me. In my mind and heart that's what I want, but in reality, when they do it, I get pissed off and end up walking away, of course, they let me go without a fight.

I get my hair braided and pinned within five minutes before walking to the closet, pulling out a pair of black pants and a cream top. I get the pants on, then button the top up before grabbing a blazer and sliding my feet into my flats.

Returning to the bathroom, I grab my vitamins and take them with my coffee. I look at myself in the mirror, taking note of the dark circles under my eyes from the lack of sleep. I ponder for two seconds on whether to put some make-up on to cover the bags under my eyes, but quickly dismiss it. I'm not a person who needs or wants to wear make-up, plus I expect everyone will have dark circles under their eyes today.

I grab my coffee cup, leave the bathroom, and make my way to the kitchen, draining the last of my cup and placing it in the dishwasher, then grabbing my travel cup and filling it with coffee before I head out the door.

I pull into the parking lot at five minutes to seven, seeing that I am the first one to arrive. I make my way into the building and up the elevator to our floor. I unlock the office and head straight to my computer to see if Public Safety has sent over the data from Uber or Lyft yet.

Just as I get into my emails, Heath and Declan walk in, both looking worse for wear.

"Did either of you get any sleep?" I ask.

Heath shakes his head no, and Declan doesn't respond.

I nod in understanding as I watch both of them make their way into the conference room to continue looking through the files of past cases.

I scroll through my emails and find the one I've been waiting for. I open the data sheets and scroll through them, looking for Kim's name or address, only to be disappointed when Eric walks in with Frankie following behind him.

"Did you get the data from Public Safety?" Eric asks me, and I nod.

"There are no pick-ups in Kim's name or from her address, nothing for her neighborhood either," I say quickly before he can ask.

He nods and walks to the conference room.

I grab my notebook, pen, and coffee, following behind Eric as he enters the conference.

He looks at the stack of files on the table, "Is this all the past cases that Kim has worked on?" he asks.

"Yes, Sir. All the ones we could find that have her name in them," Heath responds.

"Good. I want everyone to grab a few files, we are going to go through them all together. I want you to chase down where the criminals are and who their closest relative or friend is and find out what they are doing. If you think we have something potential to chase, put it in a pile in the middle of the table. Someone has Kim, and we need to find her," Eric tells the room, as we all grab files and open our laptops.

I open the first file that I grabbed. It's the first case we worked on as a team when I started. The serial killer was picking up prostitutes, killing them, and getting rid of their bodies by feeding them to his pigs. He killed over forty-nine women before we received a tip that led to his arrest. Looking up the suspect, I see he's still in prison, though he was attacked a couple of weeks ago and is currently listed in critical condition. No family and no visitors. "I hope he dies," I mutter.

"Huh, what?" Heath asks.

"Nothing, we don't need to worry about this one," I say, throwing the file into the discard pile and grabbing another.

I look up the next serial killer, his family, friends, and visitors, and again nothing jumps out as a possible person who would have a vendetta against Kim or the team.

For the next three hours, we all go through the files. The discard pile is larger than the potential pile. We are so engrossed in what we are doing that the ringing of Eric's cell phone has us all jumping.

I watch as Eric looks at the caller ID, giving off a confused look, before answering and walking out of the conference room, presumably going to his office to handle the call.

I decide now is probably a good time to take a break. The coffee has long since been gone, and I need something else to drink. I stand up, and my legs feel like jello from sitting too long, it takes me a few minutes to get the blood moving again before I move and make my way to the bathroom. Once I return, I grabbing a bottle of water from our refrigerator.

Eric comes back to the conference room as I sit back down.

"Mya, I need you and Heath to go to Boston," Eric says.

"Why do we need to go to Boston?" Heath asks, sounding irritated.

"The Boston Field Office called, that was Agent Anderson on the phone, seems Boston Homicide may have stumbled onto a serial killer."

"Well, if it's in Boston, why are we being called in and not the Boston Behavioral Unit?" Heath asks. "Don't they know we have an agent missing?"

"I told him, but it seems the killer is getting on the train here in Maine and killing a man and woman on the train before it pulls into Boston," Eric relays. "They feel it falls under our justification," Eric says.

"A man and a woman?" I ask.

"I have printed all the details," he says, passing over the files. "You will need to get with Detective Shane Maguire and his partner, Detective Nora Riley. Here is their contact information," he answers, handing me a piece of paper. "I suggest you get there as soon as possible and assess what you can," Eric adds.

"What about Kim?" Heath asks.

"We will continue looking for her, but in the end, we also still have a job to the people, and if there is a serial killer, it's our job to find them," Eric tells him.

I grab my laptop, notebook, and pack them into my case to take with me.

"Let's go, Heath, the sooner we get there, the sooner we can get back and continue looking for Kim," I tell him as I grab my case.

"Fine," he says with a huff.

"Call me and let me know what you find out," Eric commands, and I nod before grabbing the key to our government car and walking out of the office to the elevator.

Heath and I get in the car, with me driving the four hours to Boston.

"I can't believe we have to go deal with someone else's case while we have a team member missing," Heath whines.

"I get it, it's bad timing," I start.

"Bad timing? We shouldn't even be involved in this. Kim should be the most important case right now. What if she's been hurt? How can Eric think this is okay?"

"Listen, Eric, Frankie, and Declan, plus Michelle will continue looking for Kim. We still have a job to do, so if that means dividing in order to complete both cases, then that is what we are going to do. Let's just hope this case doesn't take us long so we can get back and help, but I know the team is not going to rest until we have Kim back, and you need to believe that too."

"But what if they need extra hands or eyes for something?"

"If Eric needs us, he will call. As it is right now, we have no leads to where Kim is or who could have her. We need to trust the team to find leads, and they need to be able to trust us to solve this case for them."

"I know you are right, but everything feels wrong," he says.

"I know. We've never worked a case without the whole team before," I begin.

"No, we haven't," he says. "Do you think Boston could have a serial killer coming from Maine?"

"Anything is possible, but until we hear all the details, it's very hard to conclude right now, though I wouldn't be surprised. Kim did say Maine is a breeding ground for serial killers because they can get lost in the area," I answer.

I watch as he nods, and then I hear, "I'm worried about Kim," Heath says quietly.

"Me too," I whisper. "Hey, why don't you read the files so we have an understanding of what we are walking into," I tell him, trying to refocus his thoughts for the time being.

Chapter Four

SHANE

The crime scene techs found the male victim's briefcase and the female's purse. With the wallet that the coroner found on the male victim, we were able to identify both victims and find the next of kin.

The female was Jessica Leery. She was single, her mother and sister were listed as her emergency contacts. We opted to notify the mother, who lives locally, while the sister lives in New York. The male was Mr. George Bridden, he has a wife and two kids here in Boston and was the CEO of Val Corp, a tech company, and Ms. Leery was his secretary.

Nora and I pull up to Mrs. Leery's house first to make the notification. It's a small little cottage that you don't see many of these days. There is a small porch, and I take in the light blue door as Nora and I walk up to it. I knock on the door, and we wait just a few seconds before the door is opened by an older woman with dark hair pulled back.

"Mrs. Leery?" I ask.

"Yes, can I help you?"

"Ma'am, I'm Detective Shane Maguire, and this is my partner, Detective Nora Riley. May we come in and speak with you?"

"Of course, please come in," she says, showing us into the living room. "Please take a seat. Can I get you anything? Coffee? Water?"

"No, ma'am, thank you," I say as I look around the small but spacious room. There is a couch and two high-back chairs, with a small coffee table in the middle. I look over and see a wood-burning fireplace with family photos spread out over the mantle.

On the wall behind me is a cabinet filled with all kinds of knick-knacks, and in front of me is a bay window looking out toward the street.

Once she takes a seat on the couch, I sit in the chair opposite her.

"Ma'am, is your daughter Jessica?" I ask.

"Yes, I have a daughter Jessica. Has something happened?" she asks.

"Can you tell us about her?"

"Oh?" she asks nervously before speaking. "Well, Jessie has always been a good girl. We lost her father, my dear husband, when Jessie was fourteen and her sister, Maddie, was eighteen. She had a hard time with the loss, but she came through it, worked hard, and graduated high school. She was accepted to Boston University and did a summer internship with Val Corp a year before she graduated. She was offered a job with the company straight out of college and was so excited."

"What does she do there?" I ask.

"She works at Val Corp as an administrative assistant for the CEO."

"How long has she worked for Val Corp?" I ask.

"About five years now," she replies. "Is she in trouble?" she asks worriedly.

"What can you tell me about her boss?" I ask instead.

"Mr. Bridden? She seems to enjoy working for him, never had a bad thing to say about him," she tells me.

"When was the last time you spoke to Jessica?" I ask.

"Yesterday. She and her boss took the train to Largo, Maine, on Friday for a weekend business conference, and she called to tell me she would be back today. "What is going on?" she asks again more forcefully.

"Mrs. Leery, I'm sorry to inform you, but there was an incident on the train, and your daughter didn't survive," I tell her softly.

"What? What are you talking about?" she asks, tears filling her eyes. "My Jessie is gone?" she inquires quietly.

"Yes, ma'am, I'm so sorry," Nora tells her as she sits down beside Mrs. Leery, holding her hand.

"I don't understand. What happened?" she asks as the tears flow down her face.

"She and her boss, Mr. Bridden, were both attacked on the train, and neither survived," I tell her without going into too much detail.

"I just spoke to her yesterday, and she sounded so happy," she whispers in disbelief over the news we have just given her.

"Is there someone we can call for you?" Nora asks her softly.

Mrs. Leery shakes her head. "I'll call her sister myself," she says, as her body wracks with sobs.

Mrs. Leery reminds me a bit of my mom, and to see her like this is devastating. Even though I know there is nothing I can do, a part of me wishes I could take her pain away. Instead, I hand her my card and say, "The number on the back is to the morgue. You can call them and tell them what funeral home you will be using for Jessica once you figure that out, and my number is on the front if you have any more questions.”

“Thank you,” she says through her cries.

Nora and I leave her to her grief as we make our way to the Bridden residence to inform another family.

We pull up to the address that was on the driver’s license, and I take in the influential neighborhood. The house is massive and white, with very little brick as an accent. By the looks of the outside, it’s at least five thousand square feet and a minimum two-story home. The yard is well manicured, and I would not be surprised to learn they have a gardener who keeps up with the maintenance.

Nora and I make our way up to the door. There is no front porch, so I knock on the white door, and we wait.

A woman with blond hair cascading down over her shoulders, dressed in a pantsuit, answers the door.

“Can I help you?” she asks.

“Are you Mrs. Bridden?” I ask.

“Who are you?”

“I’m Detective Shane Maguire, and this is my partner, Detective Nora Riley. We would like to speak with Mrs. Bridden,” I answer politely.

“I’m Mrs. Bridden, but please call me Laura,” she says before adding, “What can I do for you, Detectives, today?”

“Ma’am, can we please come in?”

“Has something happened?” she asks, concern showing in her voice.

“Yes, ma’am, can we please come in and speak with you?” I ask again.

“Yes, I’m sorry, please come in,” she says as she opens the door wider, allowing us access to her home.

Walking in, there is a vast difference between the Leery home and this one. Where the Leery home felt comfortable and warm, this one feels cold. All the walls are stark white, the decor feels expensive and looks flashy.

Mrs. Bridden leads us into the sitting room, where the furniture doesn't look to have been sat on. The room, though nice looking, feels like an interior designer did the room.

"What has happened?" she asks, turning to us as we walk into the room. Since she did not offer for us to take a seat, Nora and I continue to stand.

"Ma'am," before I could say anything else, two children come running into the room, calling out for their mom.

"Mom, Mom, look what we did," they both say excitedly before coming to a stop in the room when they see Nora and me.

"Children, we have company," Mrs. Bridden bristles at them before calling out, "Mrs. Norris?"

An older lady walks into the room, wearing what could be considered a maid's outfit. "Yes, Mrs. Bridden?" she asks.

"Please take the children to the playroom and tell Mrs. Donovan I will be speaking with her later," she grits out.

"Yes, ma'am. Come children," Mrs. Norris says softly before leading them upstairs.

"I apologize for the interruption of my children. Now, you said something has happened?" She sounds like she's asking, but her face doesn't look like she's asking.

"Ma'am, I'm sorry to inform you, but your husband was attacked on the train this morning coming in from Largo, Maine, and he did not make it," I tell her.

"I see. Was anyone with him?" she asks.

"Yes, ma'am, his assistant, and she didn't make it either," I tell her.

"His assistant," she says with a laugh. "You mean his mistress."

"Ma'am?" I ask questioningly.

"Oh, you weren't told? Yes, my husband was having an affair with his secretary, how cliche, right?" she says with a laugh as she walks the sitting room and goes to stand in front of the fireplace.

"What makes you think your husband and his assistant were having an affair?" I ask.

"She's not his first," she says simply with a shrug.

I look over at Nora, not sure how to respond to the coldness in her voice or demeanor.

She looks at her watch, then says, "I apologize Detectives, but I have a meeting in thirty minutes that if I don't leave now for, I will be late, and I despise being late for anything," she tells us as she walks back toward the front door.

"Yes, ma'am. Here is my card, the number to the morgue is on the back. Once you have a funeral home in mind, just let the coroner know, and he will ensure your husband is transported properly. If you have any questions, please don't hesitate to call," I tell her.

She takes the card, looks at it, then says, "Thank you. I wish you both a good day," as she opens the door, allowing us to walk out.

Nora and I get back in the car, and as I start it up, I say, "Wow, that was..."

"Odd," she finishes for me.

"Yeah," I breathe out. "She didn't seem upset at the fact that her husband was killed."

"No, not at all. I guess if he really was a cheater, though she probably feels she lost him a long time ago," Nora says, and I nod before putting the car in gear and driving back to the precinct.

We get back to the precinct, and Commander Doyle is waiting for us as we walk in.

"Mcguire, Riley, your back, good. Meet in the conference room now," he says, as he turns and walks toward the conference room, looking annoyed and yet relieved at the same time.

I look at Nora, and she shrugs her shoulders, following behind the Commander. I sigh as I follow them both.

Walking into the conference room, I'm stopped dead in my tracks. There are two people standing at the table, one male and one female, both dressed in suits. The male is shorter than me with dark hair, and the female is shorter than him, probably about five-five, maybe five-six. She has brown hair that is braided and pinned, so I can't be sure how long her hair is, but that's not what stops me in my tracks, it's her eyes. They are as blue as the sky without a cloud in them.

I can't help the immediate attraction I feel, it's like an invisible current is pushing me toward her, though I'm standing stiff as a board by the door.

"Agents, this is Detective Nora Riley and Detective Shane Maguire," I hear the Commander say, and it pulls me out of my trance long enough to shake some sense into myself.

I move a little bit away from the door but stay close to the wall. I nod in greeting as my mouth doesn't want to open.

"Maguire, Riley, these are Agents Robertson and Morgan from the Maine Behavioral Unit," Commander Doyle says as introductions, pointing each out. "I'll leave you four to get acquainted," he says before stepping out of the conference room.

"Is he always so pleasant?" Agent Morgan asks quietly.

I hear Nora chuckle as she says, "Sometimes."

I watch as Agent Morgan gives Nora a smile, and I'm completely struck by the way her eyes light up from that one small gesture. Her beauty is something I have only read about in books.

I'm still staring as Agent Morgan takes a seat and opens the files, then she looks up at me and says, "Do you mind walking us through each murder?" Her voice is soft with a melody that is like music to my ears. I feel pulled to her like she is the pied piper playing a pan flute, but instead, it's her voice that has me in a trance.

For one second, I'm pulled to her, but then her words register, and for some reason, I get upset, and without thinking, I say, "Did you not read the reports we sent?" I growl.

Chapter Five

MYA

The minute he walks into the room, it feels like all the air leaves my lungs. He's tall, at least six feet, muscular, with brown hair that I want to run my fingers through and see if there is enough for me to tug on. My eyes lock onto his dark blue ones, and I immediately feel a pull to him.

The Commander seems a little rough as he makes the introductions, and I notice he couldn't leave the room fast enough. I make a comment, but Detective Riley relieves my anxiety a bit by laughing, and I can't help but smile.

I know I need to sit down before I make a fool of myself, so I grab the nearest file to me, trying to feign business, and ask softly, "Do you mind walking us through each murder?"

His response was not what I was expecting.

"Did you not read the reports we sent?" he growls at me. Like he really just growled at me, and it has my back straightening.

"Excuse me?" I ask, with a bite in my tone.

"Oh shit," Heath whispers out.

I watch as Nora's face falls from her partner's gruffness. "Shane, what are you doing?" she asks in a whisper.

He ignores his partner, still looking at me. "You have the files in front of you, so why didn't you already read them? Or do you think you're too pretty to read, and we should do all the work for you?" he asks between gritted teeth.

I silently seethe inside but refuse to give this man the satisfaction of knowing he has gotten to me. I close the file calmly and gather them all up.

"We did read the files on the way down," Heath quickly jumps in. "Well, I read them, and she listened, as she was driving," he adds.

"It doesn't matter if we read the files or not," I start, "Reading something put on paper does not give the whole story. We want to hear directly from you what you saw, but since you seem to be too busy to give details, Agent Robertson and I will do our own assessment, and I'll be sure to let your Commander as well as the FBI Field Office here know just how helpful you were," I say, seething mad, but keeping my composure and words soft.

I look at the Detective, who makes my heartbeat fast, but my blood boil, and add, "If you didn't want our help, you shouldn't have called. Our time and resources would have been better used at home looking for our missing colleague."

The man may look gorgeous as hell, but he is like every other man I have ever met in his position who thinks women are only in this job because of their looks. I can't help the disgust that crosses my face at the thought.

I walk out of the conference room, and I hear Heath mutter something, but I can't make out what it was before he is walking beside me, and we are headed to the front doors.

"Are you okay?" he asks in a whisper so as not to alert anyone to what has just happened.

"I'm fine," I say, calmly walking across the parking lot to our car.

"If you say so," he says, then asks, "Where are we going first?"

"Let's go check into the hotel, then we can go over to the train station and take a look around for ourselves," I tell him.

"What do you think that was all about back there?" he asks, getting into the passenger seat.

"I don't know. I can't believe he growled at me for asking a simple question," I say.

"Right. I mean, the man is sexy as hell, and normally I would love for a man to growl at me, but that..." he says, and I interrupt.

"Do not bring up sex right now, Heath."

"Whoooo, Hunny, I was just going to say even that growl was uncalled for and a bit scary," Heath finishes, and I sigh.

"I know," I tell him.

"I will say, I did think you were finally going to lose your composure with him when I heard you snap at him. I don't think I've ever heard you use a tone other than soft with anyone," Heath says.

"Something about his question and growl set me off. I can't explain it," I tell him quietly.

"I liked it, but then you pulled yourself together again. Sometimes you need to stand up to some of these assholes and let them know they can't walk all over you," he says, and I can't help but laugh.

"I guess I do like to keep the peace more. I didn't think that was the time or place, though I would like to know what the hell about my question set him off," I reply, putting the car in drive and making our way to the hotel nearby.

"I think his partner would like to know as well. She seemed very shocked by his manner, so I would say this can't be normal for him," Heath says.

"I would say it was because I'm a woman, but so is his partner. You don't think he verbally abuses her for being a woman in their profession, do you?" I ask, not helping where my thoughts are leading me.

"No, I don't think he does," he replies honestly.

"So, it's just me, great," I say sarcastically.

"Maybe it's our position with the FBI?" he says, thinking on it, and he could be right.

We get to the hotel, check-in, and take our bags to our rooms.

"I'm going to call Chris and check in with him if you will check in with Eric. See if they found any leads on Kim, please," Heath says, and I nod before walking into my room.

I quickly dial Eric's number, and he answers immediately.

"Mya, how was the trip?"

"Good, Heath and I made it here. We've spoken with Commander Doyle and his Detectives and will be going to the train station to assess the area before we watch the camera footage. Any news on Kim?"

"No, nothing yet, but we are still going through case files. The small pile we had to look further into didn't take us long to rule them out. When I have some news, you both will know immediately."

"Thanks, Boss, we would appreciate that, and we will keep you apprised of the situation here as well," I tell him.

"Good. Let me know if you need anything."

"Will do," I respond before hanging up.

As I unpack my bag and hang my clothes, my mind goes to the Detective. The way my body reacted to him when he first walked in the room, I have never felt that kind of reaction to anyone, but then he growled at me and talked about my looks. Insinuating I only have my job because of them, and that sent my walls up immediately.

I'm used to asshole men walking all over me like I'm in their way, and normally it would not bother me, but for some reason this man's words actually hurt. I don't know why I care what he thinks about me, but I do. I can feel the tears welling up in my eyes as I remember his words and the way he looked at me.

I shake my head, trying to tamper down my emotions from the ache that his words caused, when I hear a knock on my door and immediately know it's Heath.

"One second, Heath," I call out as I take a couple of deep breaths and pull myself together. I walk to the door and open it.

"Did Eric have any news?" Heath asks as he walks into my room.

"No, nothing yet, but he promised to keep us appraised," I tell him, walking over to the bed, and grabbing the empty suitcase, and placing it next to the closet.

"Oh," Heath says quietly, and I understand how he feels. I was also hoping for better news.

"How's Chris?" I ask, hoping to get his mind off the situation for a bit.

"He's good, can't wait for me to get back," he says, with a gleam in his eyes.

"So, you did the deed, huh?" I ask and watch as his face turns red. "Wait, are you blushing? Mister, I want to discuss all the details, is blushing? He must have been really good," I say with a smile.

"Are you jealous?" Heath asks.

"Hell no. I'm very happy for you as long as he makes you happy," I tell him with a genuine smile.

Heath smiles back at me, then says, "He really is that good."

I can't help but laugh. "You'll have to tell me all about it over dinner. First, let's go look at the train station and get our bearings before we decide where to eat," I say, grabbing the files.

"Then let's go," he says as he opens the door, allowing me to step out first.

We get to the train station, following signs down to the platform. When we get there, I see the yellow DO NOT CROSS tape across the train car where the murders took place. There is no officer standing guard, so Heath and I walk under the tape and step into the car. I pull the pictures of the victims up, and Heath and I begin to walk through what I see in the pictures versus what he is seeing in the car.

"The victims were sitting here," he says as he points to the two seats.

I look at the floor next to the seat and see a pool of blood. "That pool must be from his finger being cut off," I say.

"The killer was behind them," he tells me.

"How do you know?" I ask.

"The blood spurt from their necks being cut is on the back of the seats in front of them," he tells me, and I nod, having already figured that out.

"Why did the man not fight?" I ask.

"Maybe he was the first?" Heath says.

"But then the woman would have screamed, and that would have alerted the other passengers," I say, thinking out loud.

"Do you think there are two suspects?" he asks quizzically.

"I don't know," I say as I flip through the pages in the file looking for the toxicology report. "Damn," I say.

"What's wrong?"

"There are no toxicology reports," I mutter.

"You think one of them was drugged with something?"

"I don't know, and without the reports, we can't be sure one way or another," I tell him with a sigh.

"Do you think that hot Detective left them out of the reports on purpose?" Heath asks, looking at me.

"Should I tell Chris you think another guy is hot?" I ask him with a smirk before answering his real question. "I don't know if he did it on purpose or they haven't received the reports yet from the coroner, since none of the victim's toxicology reports are here."

"Maybe we should call Michelle and see if she can help us find out who the coroner here is, or we can go back to the station and ask both Detectives," Heath throws out.

"Maybe," I say, not committing to either one right now.

"Freeze. Don't move," a male voice screams, causing both Heath and I to jump. "What are you doing? No one is allowed in here."

I turn my head around and see an officer in uniform looking at us with his gun trained on us. He looks like a kid, but probably no more than twenty-five.

"I'm placing both of you under arrest for trespassing," he says.

"Chill, man, we are the FBI," Heath says, and I turn fully around to show him my badge as Heath pulls his out.

"FBI? No one told me the FBI would be coming," he says, pulling out his phone.

"Detective, this is Officer Buckley. There are two people claiming to be FBI agents here at the Train Station with badges, were you aware?"

I can't hear what the Detective is saying on the other side of the line, but I hear the officer say, **"Yes, Sir.** He wants to talk to you," he tells me as he hands me the phone.

"This is Agent Morgan," I speak even though I'm pretty sure I know whose voice I'm about to hear, and my heart beats in excitement.

"Agent Morgan, this is Detective Maguire, why are you at my crime scene?"

"Doing my job, Detective, but you would have known that had you not been rude."

"I don't want you going on the train until I get there," he says bossily.

"I'm sorry, but you're too late for that order, Detective. Agent Robertson and I have already done our investigation of the scene. You should really make sure your officers stay at their post if you didn't want anyone coming into the scene without you," I tell him pleasantly, but inside I'm smirking, as I continue, **"We've already finished our preliminary evaluation, but I would like to know where we can get the toxicology reports since those seem to be missing from the files you sent us."**

"I'll call Max and see if he has them ready to send over," he tells me gruffly.

"Perfect, we will come by the station in the morning and pick up our copies," I tell him before handing the phone back to the officer, who looks pale right now.

"Let's go," I tell Heath, and we make our way off the train and back onto the platform. I can hear the officer telling the Detective how he only ran to the bathroom and was gone not even five minutes.

I know he was gone longer than that, since we were in the car for ten, but no need to dime him out completely.

"You enjoyed that, didn't you?" Heath asks.

"What?" I look up at him, feigning innocence.

"Letting that Detective know he's not needed," Heath says with a chuckle, and I can only shrug my shoulders.

I will never admit how much I enjoyed it, or how the sound of his voice gave me goosebumps all over.

"Let's go eat," I say out loud instead.

Heath chuckles as we walk from the platform back up to the station and out the door.

Chapter Six

UNKNOWN

I watch as the young officer walks away, probably going to find a bathroom. I need to get back on that train. I think I dropped the cap to my needle as it wasn't in my bag with the needle.

Before I can walk to the car, I see two people in suits walking down the stairs, a female and a male. I briefly see the badge glisten off the male's waistband as his coat moves, and I know they are law enforcement.

Standing here in the shadows on the platform, I know they can't see me, and I watch as they go under the tape and climb into the car. Wanting to get closer so I can hear what they are saying, I quickly sneak into the car that is to my right. As quickly and as quietly, so as not to alert anyone to my presence, I make my way through the cars until I'm standing right outside the car they are in.

I listen to how they are trying to decide if the murders were committed by one or two people. *Do they really believe it would be so hard for one person to commit the murders?* I think to myself.

The female says something about a toxicology report before the uniformed officer shows up. I watch as both the female and male jump at his screech to freeze. I won't lie, I also jumped as I was invested in what they were saying that I completely forgot about him.

As they talk to him, I silently move back away from the car door. When I look down, I see the cap I was looking for and pick it up, taking the same route out that I took in, I get back to the platform to hide in the shadow again.

I watch as the male and female exit the train without the officer. The female says, "Let's go eat," while the male chuckles.

I watch them walk up the steps, back to the station, and then see the young officer come out of the car looking flustered. Poor guy probably had his ass handed to him.

I sigh deeply, knowing I found what I came for. Thank goodness the cops here are inept to do their job properly. They only focus on the scene, not the surrounding area. I slide against the wall, keeping to the shadows, and make my way to the bus terminal that is down the other way.

I need to get back and feed my guest. I don't know how long I will be able to keep her since I know her grandfather has elicited help from the local PD and New York's PD to try to find her. Her face has been all over the local news as missing.

The question is, what to do with her?

Chapter Seven

SHANE

I end the call with Officer Buckley, dropping my cell phone down on the desk and rubbing my face with my hands. I'm furious that the FBI Agents went to my crime scene without me, but I'm more furious that Agent Morgan again put me in my place.

When the agents left the precinct, Nora looked at me and said, "What the hell was that all about?"

"I don't like the fact that they came in here not prepared and expected us to tell them everything, when all they had to do was read it in the file," I tell her, still pissed off.

"As the male agent said, he did read the files while they were driving, and she wanted to hear it from our point of view, I see nothing wrong with that. We ask families to tell us about victims in their words all the time," Nora says.

"You think I was wrong?" I ask her.

"Absolutely. You growled at her, I have never heard you do that to anyone before," she tells me.

She's got a point, I have never done anything like that, ever.

"Why would you bring up her looks? That was very degrading, you would never have tolerated anyone saying something like that to me," she says as she looks at me with disgust.

"You are right," I say with a sigh, "I don't know what possessed me to say something like that. That was very unprofessional of me, and I have no excuse for that, I will apologize."

She looks at me quizzically before saying, "Are you interested in her?"

"What? No. I just don't like the idea of someone coming in here, taking over our case, but expecting us to do the work for them," I tell her adamantly.

"Yeah, sure," she says before walking toward me. "I don't think you're being honest with yourself, plus, they didn't ask to come, we had them called in. As you heard, they have a missing colleague that they could be spending their time looking for, and instead, they are here to help us."

"Maybe we don't need her help," I say, frustrated.

"Her? So, you are interested," Nora says with a smirk.

"What? Huh? No, I already told you that," I say defensively, but Nora walks out of the conference room with a smirk.

A part of me had hoped the Agents went back to Maine, I was not prepared to hear they went to my crime scene, but I shouldn't be surprised. Agent Morgan looks like someone who needs to prove a point. I'm sure my comment about her looks didn't help.

Right now, I'm pissed that I forgot all about the toxicology reports from the last four victims, and it was Agent Morgan that reminded me in her sweet voice that has my cock rock hard right now.

I sigh again as I sit back in my chair, looking across my desk to Nora's empty one. I sent Nora home about thirty minutes ago. She looked exhausted and was still a little pissed off at me, though hopefully after some sleep, she won't be so upset with me tomorrow, especially since she's right.

I am interested in Agent Morgan, and I don't want to be interested in her. She's FBI, and she lives in Maine. Long distance anything never works, but there is something about her that calls to me and has me thinking about the feel of her pussy around my cock.

I squirm slightly in my seat to discreetly adjust myself as I try to rid my thoughts of the beautiful, petite Agent who makes my body hum and reach for my phone to call Max.

"Detective Maguire, what can I do for you this evening?" Max asks as he answers the phone.

"Hey, Max, do you have the toxicology reports for the first four victims? I know it would be too soon to have anything on the two bodies we found this morning," I tell him.

"I just received them this afternoon and will email them over to you shortly," he tells me.

"Thank you, I would appreciate that. Anything I should be aware of?" I ask.

"Both males were injected with a neuromuscular blocking agent. This would explain why they didn't fight back," Max tells me.

"A neuromuscular drug? What is that for, and who would normally be able to obtain that?" I ask him.

"NMBA's as we like to call it for short, are used to prevent muscle movement, specifically during surgical procedures or when a person needs to be placed on a ventilator. It's a powerful muscle relaxant, and the effects are normally temporary to the

individual once the medication is stopped. Any anesthesiologist would have access to these drugs, as it's something that must be given to the patient with a doctor's approval," he tells me.

"So this isn't something someone could get off the streets?" I ask.

"Normally, no, but you know as well as I do, some things that shouldn't be on the streets are," he says with a sigh, and I know he's right.

"Thanks, Max. I appreciate the insight. I'll go by Boston General tomorrow and talk with their directorate to see if they are missing any of this drug," I tell him.

"That's a good place to start. Let me know if you need any help," he offers.

"Thanks again, Max. Have a good night," I tell him before hanging up.

I place the phone on my desk, taking in the new information that the coroner just informed me of. I never thought about what the hospitals give patients when they go for surgery. I mean, I knew they gave them something to sleep, but I never realized they give you something that causes your muscles to become paralyzed.

My email chimes, letting me know Max sent over the reports as he said he would. I open up the documents and print out three copies, ensuring there is a copy for the Agents, when they come by in the morning.

I shut down my computer, grab my keys, and head home for the night. I pull up to my house and sit in the driveway allowing my thoughts to calm down.

I take in my childhood home, it's a white cape-style home, just thirty minutes from the precinct. The yard is small and manageable with a white picket fence separating the yard from the sidewalk. It has stone stairs leading to the front door flanked by wrought iron rails on both sides.

It has a detached garage that my father converted to his workshop. It has also become a place for additional storage for me since I inherited the property after my parents passed away five years ago. The paved driveway provides room for two cars, so I see no need to change the garage.

I get out of my car and walk up the stairs to the front door. Once inside, I'm met with the stairs that lead up to the second floor. I drop my keys and wallet in the dish sitting on the console table, before walking into the living area on my right. I haven't changed much since my parents passed, but I did paint the walls in the living room to a light gray, since the windows allow for so much light, I felt a darker color wouldn't hurt.

The floors are the original hardwood floors throughout the home that I had refinished. I turn on the TV, then walk past the front door on the other side to the dining room. Everything in here is original, from the built-ins to the crown molding. Though this room hardly ever gets used anymore except as a walk-thru to the kitchen.

Walking into the kitchen, it is set up in a U shape with the gas range along the back wall, the sink under the window, and a dishwasher on the side wall, while the refrigerator and pantry is along the other side wall. There is a side door that leads outside to the deck with a grill, and small backyard surrounded by trees.

The main living level has a bedroom and an updated full bathroom just off the hall from the kitchen. That was the room my parents had used all my life. Upstairs are two more bedrooms, one of which is mine. I was able to fit a king bed in there and I currently use the other as an office. There is also a bathroom up here, then a finished basement downstairs with a full bathroom, wet bar, and laundry.

The house overall, including the basement, is almost two thousand square feet. It's not much, but it's home, and I'm happy.

I grab sandwich meat, lettuce, and condiments out of the refrigerator, placing everything on the counter to make a sandwich for dinner.

I can hear the news reporter on the TV talking about the bodies found murdered on the train. I also hear Commander Doyle give his briefing to the public. *"Practice caution and be aware of your surroundings. The investigation is still ongoing, and when we have something more definite, I will inform the public."*

I shake my head but am glad he said nothing about the FBI Agents.

I finish making my sandwich, putting all the stuff away, then grabbing a beer out of the refrigerator before grabbing my plate and walking back through the dining room to the living room.

I sit down on the couch, picking up the remote to change the channel. I have no desire to hear any more news tonight. I find a movie and settle in with my sandwich and beer. Once I'm done eating, I turn the TV off, clean up and make my way upstairs to the shower, before I call it a night and head to bed. This is the first time in a while that I will be in bed before midnight, and I know I need the sleep.

My dreams are plagued with sky-blue eyes and luscious pink lips. She's on her knees, looking up at me, before wrapping her warm, silky mouth around my throbbing cock. One lick of her soft tongue, and I almost come immediately.

"Oh God," I moan as she continues to push my cock further into her mouth, hitting the back of her throat, causing her to gag, but she doesn't stop. She hollows her cheeks even more as she continues to suck on me.

I place my hand on her head, pushing her down a little more, loving the feeling she is giving me right now as she continues to stare up at me, enjoying my moans.

"Damn baby, you look so good sucking my cock," I whisper to her, and she moans, causing vibrations to zing through my cock to my balls.

"Fuck," I call out, "So good," I tell her, closing my eyes and enjoying the pleasure she is giving me.

I'm so close, I can feel my spine tingling and my balls tighten up, I need to come.

I wrap my fingers in her hair, and I thrust my hips up as I push her head down, needing to come in her mouth.

She continues to suck and gag as I pick up the pace and continue thrusting into her mouth, needing to feel the release until I finally explode in her mouth. There's so much cum, that it starts to dribble from her mouth down her chin, mixing with her saliva, but she continues sucking me clean.

I wake with a start, "What the hell?" My breaths come out in pants as if I really did have sex. I feel wetness in my sweatpants and quickly realize I came in my sleep. I hadn't had a wet dream since I was a teenager, dreaming about Mrs. Jacobs from Science class as she wore her lab coat and glasses that made her look like a hot librarian.

"Shit, I'm fucked," I whisper before getting up to take another shower.

Chapter Eight

MYA

When Heath and I returned to the hotel after dinner, he went to his room to call Chris, and I went to mine, taking a shower, and now sitting on the bed going through the files that the Homicide Division sent us.

I know I had Heath read them to me on our drive, but now I do a deep dive into the reports. Hopefully in the morning, Detective Maguire will have the toxicology reports for us. As I read the reports, I also look at the pictures that were taken of the crime scenes.

Each of the males had their ring fingers cut off, and both the females and the males had their necks sliced. Reading the autopsy reports of the first four victims, there were no hesitation marks. This was done by someone with knowledge and skills.

I read through the reports on the victims themselves and see that each of the males were with their secretaries, coming back from a conference or meeting held in Maine.

"The question is, were they really there for meetings, or were they having affairs?" I ask myself as I jot the question down on my notepad.

I look at the companies listed for each of the male victims and send an email to Frankie.

Frankie,

Could you speak to someone at IFSys and confirm if Mr. John Barber attended a meeting or conference there for the weekend of 28-30 April?

Also, speak with someone at FD Banking and confirm if Mr. Jonathan Grisholm attended a meeting or conference for the weekend of 12-14 May.

Any news on Kim?

Mya

I click send and sigh deeply. I look at the clock and see it's after midnight. I know I need to get some sleep, but I have so much running through my head, not just with this case and Kim's disappearance, but also a gorgeous asshole Detective.

I don't understand why he affects me so much, but thoughts of him have my body humming with need and excitement. I can only hope he has a better attitude tomorrow, but even I have to scoff at the thought.

I gather the files, place them on the desk, and get into bed. I turn off the light but lay in the dark with my eyes open and my mind playing out different scenarios of the blue-eyed detective.

I roll to my side, trying to shut off my mind to stop the ache that is forming between my thighs.

I take some deep breaths to calm my body down, and then close my eyes. I will myself to go to sleep.

I wake up a few hours later feeling hot and needy. My dreams were filled with the hot detective, so much so that I need another shower. Turning on the hot water to wash the remaining images from my mind, I step under the spray and allow the tension to leave my body. I wash up quickly, wanting to get some coffee.

Once I'm dressed, I look at the clock and see it's six am. I walk out of my room, next door, and knock on Heath's door.

He opens it swiftly with a smile, "Good..." He stops and looks at me. "Did you sleep last night?" he asks, concern lacing his voice, causing his smile to disappear.

"I got a couple of hours. I was reading through the files until after midnight," I tell him, honestly. "Why? Do I look that bad?" I ask, suddenly feeling self-conscious.

"You don't look bad. You never look bad," he says, overly complimenting the look part, "But I can tell you didn't get much sleep. Did you hear anything about Kim?" he asks as he closes his door, and we make our way down to the lobby for coffee and breakfast.

"No," I reply in a whisper. "I did send Frankie an email asking him to look into two companies, and I also asked about any updates on Kim, so hopefully, we will hear something this morning when they get into the office."

He nods, as we both make our way to the coffee station. I'm hoping the caffeine will help me look less tired before we get to the station.

We both snag a little table in the corner before going to look at the complimentary breakfast. I opt for a bagel, cream cheese, and a hard-boiled egg.

Heath comes back to the table, his plate filled with pancakes, sausage, bacon, eggs, and a yogurt cup.

I can only shake my head as I take a bite of my bagel.

"So, why do you want Frankie to check into companies," Heath asks before taking another bite of his pancakes.

"The first two males were employees of those companies and according to the reports, were there for either meetings or conferences. I just asked that he investigate them and see if there were actual meetings or conferences."

"You don't believe there was?" he asks.

"There very well could have been, but I don't believe that was their only purpose there. Both males took their very young and pretty secretaries with them for the weekend, and both had their ring fingers cut off, but the reports say nothing about any wedding rings being found at the scene or on the males."

"So, you think whoever killed them, may have taken the wedding rings because they were cheating?"

"I don't know. All I have right now are hunches and theories to work until they are disproven," I tell him as I sip my coffee.

"It's a good theory," Heath says, getting lost in his food and thoughts.

I look over at the TV that is on a news station. They are talking about the murders on the train yesterday, and Commander Doyle is standing outside the precinct speaking with the reporters. *"Practice caution and be aware of your surroundings. The investigation is still ongoing, and when we have something more definite, I will inform the public."*

I notice he did not mention us, and I appreciate that. If the killer knew we were involved with the case, they may go into hiding.

The news reporter continues saying, "Boston missing person's division is still looking for the missing teen from Maine, Rayeanne Burton, whose last known location was the Boston train station. Anyone with information regarding her whereabouts is advised to contact Detectives at 617-333-4442." They have her picture up on the TV.

"Detective Burton still hasn't found his granddaughter?" Heath asks.

"I guess not," I say with a sigh as I continue sipping my coffee.

My heart hurts for that family, and I can only hope they find her safe and soon.

Heath and I refill our coffee cups, then go back to our rooms to gather our things before heading to the precinct. If I'm being honest, I'm hoping Detective Riley is there, but not Detective Maguire. I would much rather get the toxicology reports from her and not see him, especially after my dreams about him last night.

I have a feeling I would not be able to keep from blushing, and I don't want this man to know that he affects me in any way.

Heath knocks on my door, pulling me from my thoughts, and I grab the files and my laptop case before opening the door to meet him.

"You got everything?" he asks, and I nod.

"Let's go deal with the devil," I mutter, and he chuckles.

"Today will be a better day," he says.

"From your lips to God's ears," I respond, hoping he's right.

Heath and I pull up to the precinct, and I do my best to square my shoulders, dreading going in there.

"Oh, look, it's McHotty," Heath says with a grin.

"Huh?" I ask before catching sight of Detective Maguire walking from the other direction.

"Well, he's no Martin Henderson, though they kind of resemble each other some during his Grey's Anatomy days, but he's still hot, so I nicknamed him McHotty since his last name is Mcguire," Heath says with excitement in his voice. "Good morning, Detective Mcguire," Heath says, smiling brightly at the man.

The detective looks up and catches my eyes. I can feel the air leave my lungs as he looks me up and down before his eyes settle on my lips. Then as if he was shocked by something, I watch as his eyes harden, and he continues to walk to the door of the precinct.

"Oh, darn, and I thought today was going to be a better day," Heath says. "Oh well," he adds, and I can't help the chuckle that leaves my lips.

McHotty, as Heath has nicknamed him, opens the door, allowing us in first, and that shocks me, but still, he says nothing as he follows behind me.

I see Detective Riley sitting at her desk, and when she looks up, she gives us a small smile before standing up.

"Good morning, Agent Robertson and Agent Morgan," she says.

I mumble, "Good morning," as I take her in. Her clothes hang loosely off her body, and I wonder if she has lost a lot of weight, or just unable to find clothes that fit her. She's about an inch taller than me, and I stand at five-five. She has blond hair that is pulled up in a ponytail, and her eyes are bloodshot and puffy, which makes me wonder if she is sleeping at all.

McHotty walks past us to his desk, grabbing something before coming back over and handing me the papers.

I look at them and see it's the toxicology report I was hoping we would get. I look over the results for the men and whisper, "They were paralyzed."

"Huh?" Heath and Detective Riley ask.

"The males had neuromuscular blocking agents in them. Meaning they were paralyzed before they were killed," I say, looking over the female's toxicology reports. "But the females were not," I say as I continue to read the reports.

"So, it could be one killer," Heath says.

"Yes, it could be," I respond, still looking at the reports.

"Excuse me?" McHotty, I mean, Detective Maguire asks.

"Can we sit in your conference room?" I ask Detective Riley.

"Sure," she says, looking confused herself, but leading us to the conference room.

I take a seat, spreading the toxicology reports out on the table so I can read them better.

"What is this about one killer?" Mcguire asks.

Instead of answering his question, I ask him, "How many killers did you think you had?"

He looks at me shocked, so I continue. "When we looked at the scene yesterday, we weren't sure if we had one killer or two. If the female had been killed first, why did the male not fight? If the male had been killed first, the female would have screamed, alerting the other passengers, so the question was, how were they killed? Could one person have done it? That's why I needed the toxicology report. Now we know, by this," I say, holding up the report, "That one person could have done it, paralyzing the male first, killing the female, then killing the male."

McGuire and Riley look pale, and then she speaks. "We never considered there could be more than one suspect."

Mcguire runs his hands down his face, "No, we didn't. We were always working on the theory that it was one, and never once took into consideration the variables of the situation."

He looks a bit humbled right now, but I don't gloat, since both of the Detectives look like they haven't gotten much sleep in months.

"How many homicide cases are you both working?" I ask softly.

"Twenty," Riley tells us.

"Then don't beat yourself up for not thinking to question a scene when your mind is also on the other seventeen cases that don't involve a train," I tell them.

I open my laptop to see if I received a response from Frankie about my inquiries, so far nothing yet.

"Want to tell them your other theory?" Heath asks.

I sigh heavily before saying, "I have asked a colleague of ours to go to the companies in Largo that these men were supposedly at either for a meeting or conference and find out if there was such an event."

"Why?" Mcguire asks.

"Because they both took their very young and pretty secretaries, and they both had their ring fingers cut off, but nothing in the reports tell me anything about their wedding rings. So the question is, were they having an affair with the secretaries?" I ask.

"The question had crossed our minds, especially since this last victim's wife confirmed yesterday that he had multiple affairs with his secretaries in the past, and she was sure he was sleeping with this one as well," Mcguire admitted.

"Then our pool of suspects just got larger," I say.

"How so?" Riley asks.

"Normally most serial killers are men, however in some cases, they can be female, and here we have a drug that's injected, which speaks female, but the slice of the neck and finger with no hesitation marks, speak male. You could be looking for anyone at this point, but whoever they are, they must have some medical background in order to know what they need and not be afraid to use a knife or scalpel," I tell them all.

"I was going to go to the hospital to talk with the director about the drugs, would you like to come along and assess the doctors?" Detective Mcguire asks me, and for a moment, I'm in shock.

"Sure, I can do that," I finally answer. "Heath, would you and Detective Riley mind going to visit the offices of the victims and see what you can find out about the two."

"We've already talked to the first set of victim's co-workers, they had nothing but wonderful things to say about each victim."

"Oh honey, no, no, no. People find out one or two of their co-workers died, they won't say anything bad or tell the truth. Especially to law enforcement, as they don't want to be the one to make the company look bad. Stick with me Hunny, I promise before the day is over, I will have all the tea," Heath says. "We are just going to need to change your outfit, you look a little out of place."

"Huh?" she asks, but Heath is pushing her out of the conference room, and I can't help the small chuckle that escapes my lips.

I look up to see Detective Mcguire looking at me. "What?" I ask, feeling self-conscious again.

"You have a nice laugh," he says, sounding shocked that he's admitting that out loud.

"Thanks," I say, feeling my cheeks heat up from the compliment, as I gather all the files and reports together.

"Are you ready to go to the hospital?" he asks.

"Yes," I say, and follow him out of the conference room.

Chapter Nine

SHANE

I lead Agent Morgan out to the car, my head reeling with how smart she really is. I didn't expect her to catch on to the paralyzing drug as quickly as she did, then her theory on possibly two killers instead of one. The thought never crossed my mind.

I was only operating on one killer, but she asked some good questions that I never even considered, and looking at it, I can't believe I didn't question how only one killer could have killed them both.

When she softly laughed at her partner and his antics, I was awestruck by the sound. She has a beautiful, soft laugh, and it makes me want to hear her full laugh.

Her phone rings, and she answers, placing the phone on speaker so I can hear as well, **"Hey Frankie, do you have something for me?"**

"I see you were working late last night," he says.

"Yeah, I was going over the case files, so did you find anything at the companies?"

"Both had a meeting on the respective Saturday's, but they didn't go past 1400, so they could have caught the train back to Boston on Saturday instead of Sunday."

"I see," she says.

"What are you thinking?"

"Did they both take their secretaries to those meetings?"

"No, it was just the CEOs of each company meeting with the president of the company," he tells her.

"Thanks, Frankie. I appreciate you looking into that for me. Anything on Kim?"

"No," he says, sounding deflated by the question.

"Shit," she says, then adds, **"We will find her Frankie."**

"I know, Mya. I just hope we find her soon," he says.

"Me too," she tells him quietly before ending the call.

"Is Kim your missing colleague? What happened?" I ask.

"Yeah. As far as we can tell, she made it home after a run at the park with some other colleagues, but when another of our colleagues got to her house to pick her up, she wasn't there. Her car, purse, and keys were, but she wasn't. Her cell phone was turned off so there's no way to locate her. She just disappeared," she whispers, and my heart constricts at the pain in her voice.

"I know you all will find her, and I'm sure you're looking at everything you can," I tell her, showing my support.

"We are. I checked all the airports, trains, and bus stations, plus called all the taxi companies, and requested the Uber and Lyft reports. Nothing. The team is combing through all our past cases, and I'm hoping they find something that will lead us to where Kim might be," she offers up.

I can't see anything that they are missing, and they all seem to be doing everything they can. So to lighten up the conversation, I ask her, "So your first name is Mya?" I really like the sound of her name as I roll it around in my head.

"Yes," she says simply.

"You can call me Shane," I tell her as we pull into the hospital parking lot and I find a space to park in.

We both get out of the car and meet at the back of the car. As we walk across the parking lot, I can feel a magnetic pull to her. I don't know why this woman affects me so much, but I find it so cute how I have to look down at her. She doesn't say anything as we make our way inside the elevator, and I wonder if she feels the same pull. I press the button, waiting for it to come to the first level. When the doors open, we both step in, and I press the top floor where the administration is located.

As soon as the doors close, the energy buzzes, and I can feel the electrical current zapping between the two of us. I can hear Mya take a sharp breath, and I want nothing more than to slam my lips on hers and feel how soft they really are. I want to taste her as our tongues battle for control.

Before I can act on my desire, the elevator door opens, and Mya quickly steps off. We walk out of the elevator and into a reception area.

"Good morning, how can I help you?" the receptionist asks.

"I'm Detective Maguire from the Homicide Division, and this is Agent Morgan from the FBI, we need to see the Director, please." I introduce us, as we both hold our badges up.

"Oh, wow, just a moment," she says, picking up the phone to make a call.

Mya and I walk around the reception area, taking in all the white furniture, green plants, and white walls. This area looks very clinical. I would expect it downstairs, and upstairs to feel a little homier.

The Director's office door opens, and out walks a man, tall with a slim build, salt and pepper hair, dressed in a suit. If I had to guess, I would say this man is in his late fifties.

"Detective Maguire, Agent Morgan," he calls out in greeting, "I'm Director Noah Fields, what can I do for you today?"

"Do you have a few minutes? I have some questions that I think only you can help with," I say to him.

"Sure, come on in," he tells us both as he holds the door open for us to enter his office.

At a quick glance, his office is huge. He has one wall of glass windows overlooking the City of Boston. He has a wall of shelves with nothing but books and a seating area in front of it.

On the opposite side of the room, against the wall, is a credenza with several filing drawers and a bookshelf attached to the top of it with pictures of his family, his degrees, and medical journals. In front of that is his massive wooden desk, with his computer, monitors, nameplate, and phone on top. In front of the desk are two chairs that he is showing us to.

Mya and I both take a seat, and Director Fields asks, "So, what can I help you with?"

"We need to know if you are able to account for all your NMBAs?"

"Of course, we can account for all our medications," he says defensively.

"Sir, I'm sure you can, however, I don't need to know about the other medications, just the NMBAs," I tell him politely.

"What is this about?" he asks, sounding annoyed that we are even here.

"Someone is using NMBAs to paralyze victims before killing them, and I need to know if you are missing any from this hospital," I tell him, slowly starting to lose my patience, but still trying to be nice.

I watch as his face goes pale at the news, then he picks up the phone. **"Gretchen, can you tell me if your department is missing any NMBAs?"**

"That's right. I need to know if you can account for all of your stock?"

"Yes, please send the report up to me as soon as possible," he says before hanging up.

"My pharmacy director will do an audit and then send the report up to me. Would you like me to send it over to you?"

"That would be greatly appreciated," I tell him, handing him my card with my email address on it.

"She should have the report to me in a couple of hours."

"Perfect, we will be waiting for it. Thank you for your time," I tell him, as Mya, and I stand up and walk out of the office.

I hit the button on the elevator, and Mya whispers, "He is hiding something, but I don't believe it has anything to do with the drugs. The man looked genuinely surprised that we were here for that."

"I agree," I say quietly so no one can hear me, just as the elevator doors open and we step inside.

"What should we do now?" Mya asks when the doors close.

"That's easy, there are nine more hospitals and three medical centers we can check with to see if any of them are missing the drug," I tell her.

"Wow, I didn't realize Boston was so big," she says in awe.

"There's more than that, but I thought we would focus on this area, and if we need to, we spread out to the other hospitals," I tell her honestly.

"Damn," she whispers.

The elevator opens, and we walk out into the lobby before walking out to the parking lot now that we have a plan.

Mya and I spend the day going to each hospital on the nearby list, with each of them telling me they would have an audit done and a report sent to us.

We head back to the precinct to see if Nora and Agent Robertson have found anything from their field trip today, and I want to check my emails to see if any of the reports have been sent over yet.

When we walk in, Nora and the Agent are laughing, and I look over at Mya, who just shrugs her shoulders.

"Heath, did you learn anything," Mya asks, and now I know the Agent's first name is Heath.

"Oh, Nora and I found out so much tea. Have you eaten yet?" he asks her.

"No, we've been visiting every hospital and medical center in the area," she says with a sigh.

"So, you didn't eat lunch?" he asks, and I feel like an ass for not thinking about getting something to eat.

"No, to be honest, I think we both forgot about food, wanting to hit every place we could before the Director's went home," she tells him honestly, and I feel relieved that it wasn't just me.

"Well, we are getting dinner because you need to eat, and Nora and I can tell you what we learned today," he says with so much excitement in his voice.

"Sounds good," she says, though I can hear the tiredness in her voice.

I wake up my computer and check my emails, so far, I have received three reports as promised, but the one I expected to see is not here, Boston General has not sent anything over. I wonder what Director

Fields is hiding. I print out the three reports I did receive and make Mya a copy for her files as well.

"Did you find out anything helpful, Shane?" Nora asks, and I can only shake my head no.

Looking over the reports of the three other hospitals, they are not missing anything, which is good to know we can cross them off our list.

"Well, let's go eat. Nora promised me a good steak house, and your boy is starving," Heath says, and both Nora and Mya laugh at him as he links his arms through theirs and leads them out of the precinct.

I can only shake my head, but a steak does sound good. I grab my keys and follow behind them.

Chapter Ten

MYA

Heath and I follow Nora and Shane to the restaurant, with me driving our car. When we got back to the precinct, I hadn't realized we never ate today as we went from one hospital to another. I just knew I was exhausted and wanted to go back to the hotel and sleep.

Being with Shane all day today was causing my body to be tense and overheated, especially in the elevators. I could feel the electrical current in the air between the two of us. At one point, I had hoped that the elevator would stop and get stuck so he would kiss me and run his hands all over my body. I know, that only happens in the movies where the girl gets stuck in an elevator with a hot guy, and it never happens in real life, but it didn't mean that's not what my mind and body wanted to happen.

I find a parking spot at the restaurant, and both Heath and I climb out, meeting Shane and Nora at the front. When we walk in, I'm surprised by the cozy feel of the place. It almost feels like home. The walls are a light color, and with the number of windows that go all the way around the building, causing the sunlight to come in, makes the inside of the restaurant bright.

There are different types of era pictures on the walls, but not so much that you are overwhelmed by the amount. One wall has a picture of a wagon train, another wall has some cowboys wrangling cattle.

As the hostess takes us to our table, I notice above us is a big wagon wheel that was turned into a chandelier. We each take a seat at the table, with Heath sitting next to Nora and across from me, leaving Shane to sit beside me. Each time he moves his arm to look at the menu, he brushes up against mine, causing my skin to break out in goosebumps.

I have a hard time concentrating on the menu, and after the fifth brush-up, I close my menu, giving up. The waitress comes over and takes our drink order. I ask for a coffee, and Shane does too, while Heath and Nora ask for alcoholic beverages.

The waitress comes back with our drinks and then takes our order, while the others are ordering, I quickly open my menu, and the first thing my eyes land on, is a six-ounce sirloin with a baked potato and salad. The waitress jots our order down and takes the menus, leaving us to finally hear about Heath and Nora's day.

"What did you learn?" Shane asks, placing his left hand under the table and brushing my leg.

I can't help the moan that leaves my lips, but thankfully, I was taking a sip of my coffee, and Heath makes a comment, "Did you not drink your fill of coffee today?"

I set my cup down, and say, "No, the last cup I had was at the hotel this morning."

"Oh, you need your fix." He turns to Nora and says, "My girl Mya has an obsession with coffee."

I can only groan.

Nora giggles and says, "So does Shane."

"So, what did you learn?" Shane asks again.

"I will say, Heath is good at getting people to talk," Nora says.

"Thanks, Babe, I knew we were going to be besties," Heath says before continuing. "The tea around the watercooler is Mr. Bridden likes to have affairs with his secretaries, and when they get too clingy, he fires them. Jessica Leery has been there the longest at five years, and word on the street was he planned to serve his wife divorce papers and marry Jessica," Heath says, taking a sip of his fruity drink.

"Oh, man, this is amazing," he says before continuing, "Anyways, some think Jessica was pregnant, but others think she was the love of his life. They say he was always smiling and happy after she came on board."

"Was that not the case before Jessica?" I ask, and Heath shakes his head.

"No, apparently, he was mean and grouchy. People hated working for him, and the only reason that the secretaries slept with him was for money. Now, how much of that is true and how much is rumor, no one can be sure, but the secretaries never lasted a year in that position."

"What did they say about Jessica?" Shane asks.

"That she was the sweetest person they ever met. She remembered everyone's birthday and anniversary if they were married. She always did something nice for everyone, and for the holidays she made sure everyone got a little something. No one had anything bad to say about her, except that she was possibly sleeping with a married man," Heath says, taking another drink.

"No one liked Mrs. Bridden, she was considered a piranha around the office. Apparently, if she came in, she would boss everyone around and was mean to everyone, including her husband," Nora says.

"That fits with the woman we met," Shane mutters.

"How can we find out if he was really filing for divorce?" I muse.

"I can check court documents and see if anything has been filed with the clerk's office," Shane responds as the waitress brings our food.

She places the steak dinner in front of me, and the aroma has my mouth watering. I cut into the steak, and it's juicy. When I place it in my mouth, the flavors hit hard, the meat is tender, and I moan like it's the best thing I have ever eaten.

"Oh my God, this is amazing," I say out loud to no one in particular as I take another bite.

I hear Nora and Heath giggle, but I don't look up. I am thoroughly enjoying this steak. Once it's gone, I can't help but pout, wishing I still had more. I take a bite of the baked potato and salad, but neither one is what I want, so I push the plates away.

"Are you finished?" Shane asks me.

I sigh, then say, "Yeah, I guess so."

"Was it really that good?" Shane asks.

"It was hands down the best meat I have ever had," I answer with a wistful look at my plate.

Heath spits his drink out, laughing so hard. Nora can't contain her laughter either, and I look at both of them like they have lost their minds.

"What?" I ask.

"Hunny, if that is the best piece of meat you have ever had, we need to find you a man," Heath tells me as he wipes his mouth and pushes his plate away.

I look him straight in the eyes and say automatically, without thinking, "I didn't say it was the best dick I ever had, just the best meat."

Shane begins to choke on his food, Nora busts out laughing even harder than before, and I can feel my face turn red.

"I'm sorry, are you okay?" I quietly ask Shane as I pound on his back.

"Umm, yeah, I'm okay," he says, and I quit pounding on his back.

I shake my head as Heath can't contain his laughter, and Nora is beside him, trying to breathe through her laughter. I could just die of embarrassment right now.

"Thanks for the clarification, Hunny bun," Heath says between his laughter.

"Glad I could clarify and entertain," I mutter.

This only makes Nora and Heath laugh harder.

When she finally gets her composure back, she says, "Thank you, this has been the most fun I've had in the last six months."

I want to ask why, but something inside me says not to bring it up, so I just nod and say, "Anytime."

I can see Shane beside me shaking his head. I have no idea what he thinks about me, but if he had any respect for me today, I'm sure that just went out the window with my comment.

Finally, the waitress comes over with our checks, and as I reach for my purse to get my wallet, Shane takes my ticket and says, "I got this."

"Thank you, but you don't have to. I mean, if anyone should pay, it should be me. I almost killed you," I tell him.

"I'm fine, and I got this," he says a little more gruffly, and I let it be saying, "Thank you."

Once the checks are taken care of, Heath and I say goodnight to both Detectives and get in our car to head back to the hotel.

"That was a fun dinner," Heath says, still laughing. "You make everything so fun, Mya."

"Me? What are you talking about? I just embarrassed the hell out of myself. I kind of forgot they were there when I said that," I tell him, as I feel my face heat up again.

"Oh, your comment was great, but I was talking about you eating that steak. You moaned the entire time you were eating. I think McHotty was getting jealous of the steak."

"What? No, he wasn't. Did I really moan the whole time?" I ask, feeling mortified if it's true.

"Yes, you did. Then when it was gone, you pouted," Heath says, laughing. "Don't worry, Mya, I think McHotty has the hots for you."

"I think you are crazy," I say softly to him.

"We already know I am, but I'm sure I'm right," Heath says.

My mind is racing with questions, but I don't allow them to show on my face. At the hotel, I park, and we make our way in and up to our rooms.

"Good night, Heath. See you in the morning," I tell him.

"Good night, sunshine," he tells me before walking into his room and allowing the door to close. I open my door, then close it. Walking to the desk and placing the files and laptop on top. I take my jacket off, placing it around the chair before walking into the bathroom and starting the shower.

I get undressed and step in, allowing the hot water to cascade over me as thoughts of McHotty evade my imagination.

I take my time lathering up my body as I imagine it's Shane's hands on me. His hands squeezing my breasts, his fingers pinching my nipples, his hand sliding down to cup my pussy and slide a finger inside, as he strokes the inside of my walls before adding another finger and finding my spot.

I allow the moan to leave me as I continue imagining that I'm riding Shane's fingers as his thumb rubs my clit in circles, before he pumps his fingers in and out of me, fucking me hard. I come so hard, but not feeling relieved. I need more.

I quickly wash up and get out of the shower. Drying off, before I put my pajamas on and climb into bed. I should have been sated with masturbating, but I'm not. My body is full of need and I'm not sure how much sleep I will get tonight.

I close my eyes, but all I see are dark blue eyes, full of desire. I haven't even known this guy for twenty-four hours. My first interaction with him, he was a chauvinistic asshole and then today he was all about business except when his hand was brushing up against me.

"God, I'm fucked," I mutter.

Chapter Eleven

SHANE

I drop Nora off at her house before I head off to mine. Thoughts of Mya fill my head, from the moans she made every time she ate a piece of steak, to her words about Dick. I couldn't help but choke as I recalled the dream I had of her sucking my cock.

What the hell is wrong with me, no woman has affected me like this, ever. Not even my ex-fiancée, who cheated on me for the four years we were together before running off with the man.

I found myself finding ways to touch her today, waiting for that electric spark to not be there, but each time I brushed up against her, I felt shocks all the way to my groin.

I get home and jump in the shower, needing to jack off, though I know it won't be enough. As soon as I feel my release, I'm still not satisfied. I know I won't be until I have her, and that can't happen. I need to get this case solved so she can go back home, and I can get back to my normal routine.

I get out of the shower, dry off, and lay in bed naked tonight. The room is dark, but I stare at my ceiling thinking about her, Mya. My brain should be focused on the twenty cases that I currently have opened, but instead, it's her blue eyes and sweet face that take up my thoughts.

"God, I'm fucked," I mutter as I roll to my side, beating my pillow to try to get comfortable.

I start to wonder if she's thinking about me like I'm thinking about her. Are the feelings I'm feeling mutual?

"What the hell is wrong with you? You barely know this woman, Jackass," I chastise myself.

I continue to curse myself until I finally fall asleep, not realizing I fell asleep until the alarm wakes me up.

⋅•◦•⋅

Two weeks later

It's been two weeks since the agents have been here. Two weeks of working beside Mya, nothing has changed. If anything, my need for her has grown. We've watched every security video from all the murders, and we are currently watching again for the third time.

"There is something we are missing," Mya mutters, and I think it's so cute how focused she gets.

Nora comes into the conference room with Heath on her heels. I look up, and she says, "The judge signed the warrant."

"Thank God," I say. Director Fields at Boston General decided he was not going to freely give us the reports and requested a warrant. We finally found a judge willing to sign off so we can get that report.

"Do you want us to give it to him, or would you like to do the honors?" Nora asks.

"I want to do it. Mya, do you want to come?" I ask her.

"Absolutely. That man is hiding something, so I say we all should go. Let's hope he didn't destroy any evidence," Mya says.

As we get ready to walk out of the conference room, Nora's phone rings.

"Detective Riley," she answers.

"Oh, is that today? I'm sorry I forgot."

"Yes, I can be there in thirty minutes, thank you."

She hangs up the phone, then says sheepishly, **"Sorry, I forgot I had an appointment today."**

"No worries, we can handle it," I tell her, and she nods.

We all leave the precinct. Nora to her appointment, and Mya and Heath with me to the Hospital.

I make sure I have the warrant in my pocket as we walk across the parking lot to the lobby. I walk up to the receptionist's desk.

"Good afternoon, could you tell me which floor I can find the director of pharmacy?" I ask her.

"She's on the sixth floor," she responds.

"Thank you," I say as I walk over the elevator and hit the button. The doors open immediately, and I punch the sixth-floor button.

We decided we would go to the source before going to see Mr. Fields.

We are led to Gretchen Fischer's office by her assistant. She's on the phone as we are standing there.

"I'm sorry, I'm going to have to call you back," she says before ending the call.

"Can I help you?" she asks as she stands up from her desk.

"Yes, ma'am. I'm Detective Maguire from Boston Homicide Division, and these are FBI Agents Morgan and Robertson," I tell her as I make introductions.

"What can I do for you?" she asks nervously.

"Two weeks ago, I was here to see the Director of the Hospital, and he called you requesting a report for your accountability of the NMBAs," I begin.

"Yes, I remember that call. I sent up the report that afternoon once the audit was completed," she says.

"Well, ma'am, we never received that report, because the Director wanted a warrant. I have the warrant, and I would like all your pharmacy audits. I will take the report you sent him two weeks ago, and I want a full audit of your entire inventory," I tell her.

"Can I see the warrant, please?" she asks, and I pull it out of my pocket. "Do you mind if I call our attorneys and have them look this over?"

"Not at all. We will be here, waiting," I tell her, and she walks to her office to presumably call the attorneys, but I think she's calling Director Fields.

My assumptions are correct when he comes storming down the hall with two suits behind him, "What is the meaning of this, Detective?" he snarls, and Ms. Fischer comes out of her office.

"Mr. Fields, so nice to see you again. You requested we get a search warrant, and that's exactly what we've done."

"You didn't come see me," he says, red-face mad.

"No, Sir. See, this warrant is for your pharmaceuticals, and that falls under the Director of the Pharmacy. We originally came to you as a courtesy, but since you wanted us to get a search warrant, this time, we came to the person responsible for the section," I tell him nicely.

"Can I see that warrant, please, Detective?" a man in a suit asks.

"Are you the hospital attorney?" I ask since he never introduced himself.

"Yes, forgive me, I'm Richard Price, one of the attorneys here, and this is Landon Marks, another attorney," he tells me, and I pass him the search warrant.

"Everything is in order, Mr. Fields, they are to have a full audit of all the pharmaceuticals in-house," Mr. Price tells him.

"What? I thought you only wanted the NMBAs?" he questions.

"I did, but you didn't want to hand that report over, so the Judge and I wondered what you could be hiding, and he agreed that a full audit of all the drugs was warranted. FBI Agent Robertson," I say, pointing to Heath, "Will be overseeing the audit to make sure the numbers aren't misconstrued. If need be, I can also bring in some guys from the crime lab to oversee as well?"

"That won't be necessary, Detective, Director Fischer will ensure everything is done accurately, and Agent Robertson can observe," Mr. Price says.

"How can this be allowed?" Director Fields shouts.

"What are you hiding, Mr. Fields?" Mya asks softly as she observes him and his behavior.

"I'm not hiding anything," he snarls at her. "We run a tight ship here, and you will find no wrongdoing here or any medications missing," he says before turning around and walking back down the hall.

"Ms. Fischer, please start the audit, Agent Robertson will follow you," I tell her as Heath moves up.

I whisper to him, "Keep a close eye on her, something is not right," I tell him, and he nods slightly.

"This could take a couple of days," Mya says.

"Hopefully, only one, but you could be right," I say as I watch them walk down the hall opposite the direction where Director Fields went.

"What should we do in the meantime?" she asks.

"We can grab some food and watch the security videos some more. You said earlier we are missing something," I tell her.

"Yeah, okay, but I'll come back later this evening to switch out with Heath so he can get something to eat," she says, still looking down the hall.

"Sounds good," knowing I'll be coming back with her.

She shoots Heath a text of the plan and we leave the hospital to grab some food to take back to the precinct.

Watching the security footage from the first murders for the fifth time, my eyes are starting to get crossed, but Mya is focused. I don't know what she is looking for or thinks we missed, but she hasn't taken her eyes off the TV screen in three hours.

"Mya," I call out to her, but she doesn't acknowledge me, still staring at the screen.

I scoot my chair closer to her, getting a whiff of her flowery shampoo. I want nothing more than to take her hair down and run my fingers through it. I close my eyes, trying to calm my raging hard-on, but allow myself to breathe her in. When I open my eyes, I see I have drifted closer to her neck. All I have to do is place my lips on it, but instead, I whisper in her ear, "Mya."

That does the trick. She jumps up screeching. "What are you doing?"

"Trying to get your attention, and that one seemed to have worked," I tell her with a chuckle.

"I'm sorry," she says, her face turning red.

"We've been looking at the screen for hours, maybe we should take a break, get some food for Heath, then we can grab something for us, before returning to this," I say, pointing at the footage.

She stretches her arms up, her white blouse pulls tightly across her flat stomach, pushing up her breasts, I want nothing more than to rip that shirt open and touch every part of her skin. She lowers her arms, grabs her blazer, and says, "Yeah, you are probably right, and I'm sure Heath is starving by now."

I turn the security footage off, grab the thumb drive from the computer, then we leave the conference room before walking out of the precinct.

We stop at a burger joint to pick up Heath some food. I grab him two combos, as the man has no issues eating.

We get to the hospital and make our way to the sixth floor. Heath directs us where to go to meet him through texts with Mya. We find him in a storage room, watching three people conduct the inventory.

"Where is Ms. Fischer?" I ask.

"She left shortly after assigning the task to these three people," he tells me.

"Here, take a break and go eat in the lobby. We'll watch them until you are done and ready to come back," Mya tells him, handing him the bag.

"Thank you. You are a lifesaver," he says and she quips back with, "I know, now go."

Heath leaves back down the hall while Mya and I watch the three technicians audit the inventory.

"Judy, could you come check this?" one of the technicians call for another.

I watch as the technician counts the vials, then looks at the paper and counts again. She looks at the technician who called her and says, "Your numbers are right, and this is a problem."

"What's the problem?" I ask.

Both technicians look nervous as they look at each other before Judy speaks up and says, "We are missing ten bottles of fentanyl tablets," she says.

"When was the last time the inventory was checked?" I ask.

"Last week," she replies, handing over the report from last week, and they are comparing it to a report of what should be here, based on what has been signed out and given to patients.

"Agent?" another technician calls out.

"Yes," Mya responds.

"We are also missing two vials of NMBAs," she says with a sigh.

"Who has access to this pharmacy?" I ask.

"Ms. Fischer, Laurel Whitney," she says, pointing to the technician beside her, "And myself, well also the Director of the hospital, Mr. Fields," Judy informs me.

"What is the procedure for getting the medication?"

"The doctor must request in the system, we get the request, then we procure and distribute it to either the doctor, nurse working that floor, or the anesthesiologist, depending on the medication and what it's for," she says.

"So, no one is authorized to procure and distribute medication, but the four names you gave me?" I ask, needing to make sure I understand.

"That is correct, Detective," she responds.

"Continue doing your audit, and make sure to mark anything else you find missing," I tell them all, and they nod and continue.

Heath comes back to the room, and we bring him up to speed.

"Ladies, how much longer do you think this is going to take?" Mya asks.

They look at each other, then look around and say, "Maybe another three hours?" Though they can't be sure and shrug their shoulders.

"Okay. I'll be back in three hours," Mya says, but Heath shakes his head.

"No. I'll call you when they are finished, and you can come pick me up then. I don't want you to come up if they aren't close to being finished."

"Are you sure?" she asks him.

"Yes. The food you brought will tie me over until morning, and I've already gone to the bathroom. I'm good," he promises her, and she nods.

"Call me, and I'll take you to breakfast before dropping you at the hotel to sleep."

He nods, and we leave him and the technicians there.

"Well, now we know for sure someone stole the medication from here," Mya says.

"Yeah, but who? Both Ms. Fischer and Mr. Fields were nervous when we wanted to do an audit. Ms. Fischer didn't even stay around."

"I agree," Mya says. "We need to find out more about them and their life."

"Want to grab something to eat and take it to my place?" I ask her before thinking.

Chapter Twelve

MYA

He just asked me if I wanted to go to his place, and I'm not sure what to say. Part of me wants to say yes, and the other part of me is struggling with, is it smart?

"We don't have to," he says quickly, almost sounding disappointed. "We can go back to the precinct if you like."

"No, we can go to your place, it's fine. I should be able to connect to the FBI VPN as long as you have WIFI. Do you have WIFI?" I ask him.

He chuckles. "Yes, I have WIFI."

"Good, then yes, we can get some food and go back to your place," I tell him, curious about how he lives.

"How does a pizza sound?" he asks.

"Pizza sounds good," I admit, and my stomach picks that exact moment to growl.

We both laugh, and I say, "Guess I am hungry."

"What kind of pizza do you want?" he asks me, and I'm sure he's not going to like what I have to say.

"I'm a pepperoni, bell peppers, pineapple, and jalapeno girl," I say, waiting for him to chastise me about pineapple on a pizza.

"Okay, got you," he says instead as we pull up to the local pizza place.

He gets out and goes into the joint as I sit in the car wondering if I'm making a mistake by agreeing to this. Do I want things to happen? Maybe. Am I being foolish to hope he does kiss me tonight? Maybe a little, but I feel like we have been tiptoeing on a tightrope around each other for the last two weeks. My dreams consist of this man every night. I guess I need to know where we stand one way or another.

He comes back into the car carrying two pizza boxes. He hands them both to me, and I hold them until we reach his house. It's a cute cape-style home.

He takes the pizza boxes from me, and I grab my laptop bag, get out of the car, and follow him up to the front door.

He unlocks it, opens the door, turns on a light, and says, come on in. He walks over to the console table, dropping his keys into the bowl on the table. He leads me through a small, but quaint dining room, and into the kitchen.

It's a nice size kitchen, set up in a U shape. He places the pizza boxes on the counter and reaches into a cabinet for plates.

"Do you have something to drink?" I ask him.

"There are some beers, cokes, and water in the fridge," he tells me.

I open the fridge and grab two beers. When I turn around, he is holding our plates in his hands.

"We can go eat in the living room," he says, a bit shyly now.

"Sure," I say with a small smile.

I follow him back through the dining room, past the front door, and into the living room. I'm surprised by how clean the place is.

"Do you live with someone?" I ask him as he sets the plates down, and I set the beers next to them.

"No. This is my childhood home. I inherited it after my parents passed away."

"I'm sorry to hear that. It must be nice to live the rest of your life in a house you grew up in," I tell him as I take a seat.

"What about your parents? Do they still live where you were raised?" Shane asks.

"They finally retired a few years ago and moved to Florida. I hear from them occasionally when they remember me," I tell him, taking a bite of my pizza.

"What do you mean?" Shane asks.

"My parents are what you would call workaholics. They both worked twelve-hour days, and I was left to my own devices," I tell him, taking another bite of pizza.

Shane says, "I'm so sorry."

I shrug because it was all I ever knew.

"It wasn't so bad. I learned how to be independent and take care of myself. I never let my grades slip, and I always did what I was supposed to, but the downfall was I could never be a kid. I wasn't allowed to go to the movies or to the mall with my friends," I say, shrugging.

"How did you join the FBI?" he asks.

"As soon as I graduated high school, to the dismay of my parents, I joined the Army, and they paid for my college. I knew I wanted to go into law enforcement and became an MP. My plan was to do four years of active duty, get my college degree in criminal justice, and then join the local PD at home, but then I got an invitation to go to Quantico. I decided it wouldn't hurt to go, so I did, and now here I am."

"So, your team is…"

"My family? Yes, they are. They are the people who have stood by me, know me, and always have my back," I tell him honestly.

"That's great that you have that bond," he says wistfully.

"What about you?" I ask him as I take another bite of my pizza.

"Like you, I joined the military, but I went into the Marines. I did four years, and when it was time to decide whether to reenlist or get out, I realized I wanted to do something different. So, I came home and joined the police force, working my way up from patrol to homicide. The department is my family, but there has been so much turnover that all the guys I came up with and respected have all left the force for one reason or another."

"What about Nora?" I ask.

"Nora is a great partner, but we've only been partners for the last three years," he tells me.

"Oh, well, what about siblings?" I ask.

"I have one sister, but she lives in Colorado with her husband and two kids. I hardly get a chance to see them, and she never comes home, not since our parents died in a car accident five years ago," he says, taking a drink of his beer.

"I'm sorry to hear that. I always wanted a sibling, but that never happened," I say softly. "Well, I guess we should look up Fischer and Fields," I say, pushing my empty plate away, and grab my laptop bag, pulling out my laptop. I boot it up and have Shane log into his WIFI, so I can VPN into the FBI System.

I run a background check on Ms. Fischer first. She's been married three times and is currently carrying $150,000 in debt.

"Oh, this is interesting," I say, and Shane asks, "What?"

"Mrs. Gretchen Fischer used to be Mrs. Fields during her second marriage. She was married to Noah Fields for ten years. I wonder if that's how she got the job at the hospital?" I say to myself, but of course, Shane hears me.

I look up Noah Fields and see the man is on his fifth marriage, paying alimony to three wives, but not Gretchen, as she is already remarried. He is currently $500,000 in debt. I look at his pay and see he is currently bringing home $150,000 a year.

"He and Gretchen could be in cahoots. She procures the drugs for him, and he sells them, otherwise, I don't see how he could afford his house, car, and the alimony payments he has to make, plus all the living expenses. It looks like his credit cards are maxed out, and I would wager a guess that is all his current wife's doing," I tell Shane.

"But do you see them as the train killer?" he asks.

"No, but if they are selling the drugs, then they are potentially selling to our killer," I say.

"Makes sense," Shane says.

I check my phone and see a text from Heath.

> **It's probably going to be another few hours, get some sleep and come get me in the morning when you wake up.**

"Well, looks like Heath is going to stay all night. He asked me to come get him in the morning," I tell Shane as I log off, close the laptop, and put it back in the case.

"Want to stay here?" Shane asks. "If you are not comfortable with that, I can take you back to the hotel," he adds.

I grab the plate and make my way into the kitchen as I wrestle with my head and body on what to do. My head says leave, and my body says stay. I rinse my plate in the sink, and I'm so torn with what to do, that I don't hear Shane come up behind me.

"Mya," he whispers in my ear, spinning me around to face him. Before I can react to anything, he slams his lips on mine, and I get lost in the feeling of our tongues battling each other.

He pulls back from the kiss and says, "Stay, please."

"Okay," I whisper because I really want to.

He lifts me up, and I wrap my legs around him as he carries me upstairs and lays me down on the bed, kissing my lips. I can feel how hard he is through our clothes as he rubs against me.

He pulls back from the kiss and stands up, unbuttoning his shirt, and I can only watch in anticipation. My mouth waters when he finally gets to the last button, and then he shrugs out of his shirt. I see he has a Celtic tattoo over his left peck, and an arm sleeve of some type of design, though I can't be sure what it is, yet.

"Wow, clothes really do hide the good stuff, don't they?" I whisper as I take in his six-pack abs.

He undoes the button on his pants, and I can feel myself getting wet. Once he unzips his pants and pulls them down, I can see he doesn't wear underwear. His cock is standing straight up and hard. I can see the precum glistening off the tip, and my mouth waters to taste him.

"Soon, love. Right now, I want to see you naked," he tells me as he pulls me up to stand and starts to unbutton my top.

I run my hands over his chest and tattoos, loving the feel of his light dusting of chest hair. I hear him take in a sharp breath, and I know it's because my hands are exploring.

He gets my shirt unbuttoned and pulls it down my arms, but doesn't take it off all the way, instead, he leans his head down and kisses the tops of my breasts that are not covered by my bra. He reaches behind and unclasps my bra, pulling the straps down to meet my shirt as he takes in my full breasts and flat stomach.

"You are absolutely gorgeous, love," he whispers to me before latching on to my nipple and sucking, as his hand fondles and squeezes the other one.

I reach down and start stroking his cock.

I feel him reach between us and undo my pants before sliding them and my panties down my legs. He kisses my stomach as he lowers my pants until his face is at my pussy.

He grabs my shirt and bra, taking them completely off and lowering me onto the bed so he can get my pants and panties off.

I feel completely exposed, but the heat and desire shining in his eyes tell me I have nothing to worry about.

He opens my legs, kissing down my thigh, breathing over my pussy, before kissing the other thigh.

My body is shaking from need when he finally swipes his tongue through my folds and up to my clit, taking it in his mouth and sucking on it hard.

My back bows off the bed from the sensation, but his hand clamps me down while his tongue enters my pussy, and he begins to fuck me.

"Oh shit," I call out.

Chapter Thirteen

UNKNOWN

I walk into the Largo train station after following my prey. The couple, like all the others, doesn't pay attention to their surroundings, they are so focused on each other.

She's a young, blond woman, full of giggles, and big breasts that are barely contained in her short dress. He's an older man, wearing a dark blue business suit. Right now, his hands are all over her ass. If he grabs her anymore, the world won't have to wonder if she is wearing any underwear, they will know.

I grab a coffee like I do each time I am here and wait for them to take a seat, then I find a seat closest to the platform, but am able to keep them in my line of sight.

The doors to the platform open, and I once again grab my bag, taking my time to get up as I watch the couple make their way out onto the platform. They go to the business car, as I stand in line for the economy car.

I watch them board before I hand my phone over to the conductor to scan my ticket and assign me a seat.

"Seat 32," he tells me, and I give him a small smile.

I board the train and take my seat, patting my bag as I smile. I have a couple of hours before I need to make my delivery, so I sit back and close my eyes. I hear the conductor as he tells everyone we will be leaving soon.

The next time I open my eyes, I look at my watch and see we are close to reaching Boston. I grab my bag, make my way to the next car, and stop at the bathroom. I pull on my black hoodie and gloves, before making my way to the next car, where I find my prey.

The young blond woman is currently bouncing on the man's cock as he thrusts in her. Her breasts are exposed as he sucks on them, while holding onto her hips. Her eyes are closed as she enjoys the pleasure he is giving, and she is taking.

"Do they really believe the people around them don't know what they are doing?" I think to myself, disgusted.

I slide into the seat behind them, neither noticing, and no one else is looking back as they can hear what is clearly going on.

I take the needle and knife out of my bag. I uncap the needle and jab the liquid into the arm of the man between the seats. Once that is done, I place the needle into my hoodie pocket, grab the knife, and grab the woman's hair.

She opens her eyes, looks straight at me, and before she can say anything, I slice across her neck. Blood spurts all over me and the man. I grab his neck next and slice, causing his blood to spurt all over the female. I quickly cut his third finger off, where the white circle, indicating a wedding band should be, is.

I grab my bag and back out of the car, going to the next one, and walking into the bathroom. I take the hoodie off, placing it in a plastic bag, knowing I will need to burn this. I cap the needle and throw it in the bag as well, before running the water, cleaning my knife and face.

I grab another hoodie from my bag, put it on, and place everything else in my bag. I can feel the train slow down, so I leave the bathroom, head back towards my car, and wait for the train to stop before debarking.

I quickly get off the train and head for the parking lot, knowing I need to get out of here before those FBI agents show up with the local police.

Chapter Fourteen

SHANE

The moment I taste her sweet juices, I'm a goner. She tastes amazing, and her body is absolutely perfect and responsive. I'm holding her abdomen down with one hand while I'm tongue fucking her and enjoying her intoxicating flavor.

I watch as she bows her back, unable to control herself. I can feel her legs start to shake, and I know she's close to her first orgasm. I want to take my time with her, but my cock is so swollen and hard.

I swipe my tongue to her clit again, sucking it in, then gently biting down on it, causing her to explode. I lap up the juices of her orgasm, and I can't get enough. I feel like a dying man getting his first taste of water in a long time.

I finish with my taste test and begin kissing up her body, needing to feel her wrapped around my cock.

"Let me taste you," she whispers.

"Next time, love. I need to be inside you," I whisper to her before taking her lips in a passionate kiss, as my cock lines up at her entrance, and I slowly push the tip of my head inside her, then pull back a little before penetrating her further.

I can feel her walls stretching to accommodate me each time I push into her. She's so tight and warm wrapped around me, and I'm not even all the way in yet.

I lean down and kiss her mouth, taking in her moans, and I push deeper and deeper until I'm fully sheathed. I rotate my hips, and she wraps her legs around me so I can go deeper still.

I'm trying so hard to stave off my own orgasm, but damn, her pussy is so tight, it's like a vice grip around my cock. I continue going slow, building her up and enjoying the feel of her body. It's better than I even imagined as our bodies start to glisten from the sweat as we make love.

I lean down and take a nipple in my mouth as her hands explore my back and sides.

"Oh, Shane, so good," she moans.

"Yes, love," I grit out, trying so hard to take it slow, when all I want is to ram into her to hit my release.

"I need more, Shane, more," she moans out, and I pick up the pace.

Kissing her deeply as I thrust into her, I can feel her walls contracting around my cock, and I know she's close. My lower spine in my back is tingling, and I can feel my balls tightening up, I'm so close, but I need her to come first.

I grip her hand in mine and hold it above her head, and I thrust into her.

"Oh, Shane, yes, more. I'm so close," she tells me, and I push deeper into her.

"Oh God," she calls out.

I moan, "Oh Fuck, love, I need you to come. I can't hold out any longer," I tell her. "You feel so fucking good," I add as I thrust inside her.

I feel her walls tighten down, and her juices flood my cock, pulling the cum from me, and I thrust hard one time, coming deep inside her as she detonates.

"MYA," I roar out as she screams my name.

"SHANE!"

We are both breathing hard, and it takes a few minutes to come back into my body. I lean down and kiss her soft lips, before slowly pulling out of her.

She winces a little but gives me a blinding smile when I pull back from the kiss.

"Are you okay?" I ask.

"Perfect," she says.

"I want to do that again, but I'm going to need rest first, love," I tell her with a chuckle.

She laughs and says, "Me too."

I pull her into me, and she lays her head on my chest and wraps her arm around my waist, as we both continue getting our breathing under control.

I lay there, knowing exactly when she falls asleep as her breathing evens out, and her body relaxes.

I kiss the top of her head. I've fallen head over heels for this woman already, but I don't know how she feels or how we could make this relationship work with me in Boston and her in Maine. I choose not to dwell on it and just enjoy being in the moment with this gorgeous woman who has brought light into my dim world.

I close my eyes and fall asleep with Mya in my arms.

I'm woken by the ringing of my phone. Mya is still in my arms, and she begins to stir as I reach for the phone. I look at the time and see it's seven am.

"Maguire," I answer gruffly.

"Shane, it's Nora. We have another couple."

Mya must hear her, because she immediately sits up and looks at me. Her full breasts on display for me, teasing me to come suck and play.

"Did you call Max?" I ask as I continue to devour Mya with my eyes.

"I did, he should be arriving soon. I'm on my way there now," she tells me. "Do you want to call the Agents, or should I?"

"Heath is at Boston General, the audit should be completed soon if you want to swing by there and get him. I'll tell Mya, and we will meet you there," I tell her.

"Sure, I can pick Heath up. See you there," she says, before hanging up.

"Another train homicide?" she asks.

I nod before grabbing her and pulling her mouth to mine for a kiss as I lay her down.

"I know we don't have time for this, love, but I need to be inside you," I tell her and watch her nod as her eyes dilate with need.

I thrust deep and begin to pound into her.

"Oh, Shane," she moans, and I do too.

"You are perfect, love," I tell her before taking her lips in a kiss and slamming my cock deep inside her.

"Faster, Shane. So. Close." She moans, and I lift her legs higher so I can pound deep inside her.

"Fuck Mya," I groan out as I continue thrusting hard and deep.

I feel her walls tighten, and then her orgasm explodes, allowing her juices to coat me so I can get even deeper.

I pick up the pace, chasing my own release, needing to come like a caveman putting a claim on his woman.

She comes again, and this time, I come with her, taking her lips in a kiss and swallowing her screams.

I put her legs down, before pulling out of her. I make my way to the bathroom and turn the shower on, before coming back into the bedroom. I pick her up and carry her into the shower.

"I'm going to have to go back to the hotel to get some clothes," she whispers to me.

"I know," I tell her as I wash her up, wishing I could take more time getting to know her body, but there is a crime scene we need to get to, even if I would rather spend the day in bed learning all her likes and dislikes.

She washes me as I wash her, but we each make quick work of the other, knowing we don't have much time.

She puts on a pair of my boxers and a t-shirt, and my heart melts more seeing her in my clothes. I drive her over to the hotel, completely turned on. I walk with her to her room, and the minute the door closes, I can't help myself.

I help her undress, then bend her over the bed and take her from behind. Seeing her wearing my clothes gave me such a hard-on that I can't help needing to feel her one more time.

I pound into her, pulling her hair, and loving her screams.

"Oh God, Shane. YES," she screams out, and I'm loving my name on her lips.

"That's right, love, I'm making you scream. I'm pounding into this pussy. It's my pussy," I tell her with every thrust that hits her in the right place. I reach around and rub her clit with one hand as I pinch her nipple with the other.

"Oh, fuck," she calls out before she detonates again, and I thrust three more times, before following her in my own orgasmic bliss.

I stand there, unloading inside her, and tell her, "I wish we could do this all day. I want to get to know every aspect of your body and your mind," I whisper to her.

"Me too," she whispers back with a crack in her voice.

I pull out of her and turn her to face me. "What's wrong, love?" I ask, seeing a sheen of tears in her eyes.

"Nothing. I'm happy. I'm happy being with you, it's just shit that we both have a job to do and right now, we are running behind," she says, walking away and going into the bathroom to clean up before getting dressed.

Once she's dressed, we make our way over to the train station with Mya being quiet during the entire ride.

I can't help myself, I grab her hand and hold it. She doesn't say anything, but I see the small smile that crosses her face. As soon as we get to the train station, I quickly kiss her hand, letting it go so we both can get out of the car.

We make our way through the station and down to the platform. Nora and Heath are waiting by the train car for us, and Officer Buckley is cordoning off the area.

"Is Max here already?" I ask, but Nora shakes her head.

"No, there was another homicide last night, so he is still at that scene, but he should be here shortly. The crime scene techs are in the car, so we opted to wait out here until they are done, given the amount of space in the cars," she says.

"Oh My God," Heath exclaims.

"What?" We all ask him in unison.

"You are glowing," he tells Mya, and I look over at her, not understanding what he's seeing since she always looks like she's glowing. My perfect Angel sent from above.

"You have the 'I've been fucked really good' glow," he tells her.

"What the hell are you talking about?" she asks.

"Who was the lucky guy?" he asks instead of answering.

Nora is looking between them confused, but then Heath says, "Oh My God, it was McHotty, wasn't it?"

"Heath, stop," Mya says, her face turning red from embarrassment.

I can't tell if the embarrassment is from being caught or because of me, and the last thought stings a bit.

"It was. Oh, Girl, you are going to have to give me the deets later," he says, then he pouts.

"What's wrong?" Mya asks.

"You were getting good fucked, while I was standing and watching three women count meds all night," he tells her, and she rolls her eyes.

"I'm sure Chris will be happy to know you spent all night with three women instead of three men," she tells him, and he can't help but nod.

"Congratulations, you two," Nora says, but I can't tell if she is truly happy about our relationship or if this is a reminder of what she once had.

"I called it. Did I not tell you, Nora, these two would be perfect for each other if they just got out of their own way," Heath says.

"You absolutely did," Nora says with a chuckle, and I relax a bit, knowing she isn't upset with us but probably really does miss her husband.

Finally, the crime scene techs complete the scene about the same time Max shows up. The five of us climb into the car and watch Max perform his preliminary, while we take in the scene before us.

Chapter Fifteen

MYA

I'm trying to assess the scene and bodies, but with Shane so close, and my body still humming from our activities this morning, he is all I can focus on.

I should have known it wouldn't take Heath long to assess and figure out what we have done. I had hoped he would be too tired to notice and would whine about needing food and sleep, but no, my co-worker/friend notices everything.

I had never felt so embarrassed to be called out as I was this morning in front of Nora.

I take in the couple, seeing the woman on the man's lap. "Wait, were they?" I begin.

The coroner says, "Yes, they were."

"That's disturbing," I say as I look around to the other seats. "I wonder how many other passengers were in the car?" I mutter.

"Eight," Nora says, looking at her notes, "And before you ask, yes, they were disturbed. They said the couple had no shame, and they weren't trying to hide what they were doing."

"I've never had sex on a train before," Heath says.

"Could you?" I ask.

"I don't know," he answers thoughtfully, as if he may actually consider it.

I look at him in disbelief.

"What? It could be a wonderful adventure. Never know unless you try something at least once," he says with a smirk, walking back down the aisle.

Nora, Shane, and myself just stare after him as we can't believe it's something he would consider.

I turn back and look at the coroner as he stands up and says, "It's the same killer. Finger has been cut off, and necks are sliced like the others. It will take some time to get the bodies out from this position."

I nod, understanding why he said that.

"But we can go get breakfast, right?" Heath chimes in, and I chuckle, shaking my head.

I knew it was a matter of time before he started to whine, later than what I anticipated, but I knew it was coming.

"Yes, we can go get you some food," I say with a smile.

"It will be a couple of hours before I can get them back to the morgue. Once I find their personal belongings, I'll call you to come pick them up at the morgue as well," Max tells Shane.

"That's fine, Doc, thank you," he tells him, and his voice causes my panties to get wet and my knees to go weak.

What the hell is wrong with me? I've had sex with this man three times, two of those times was this morning, and yet, I feel like a teenager whose hormones are out of control and can't get enough.

"First, I need to stop by the security office and get this morning's footage. Nora, why don't you and Heath head to the diner. Mya and I will get the footage and meet you there," Shane says.

"Do we have to wait for you to order?" Heath asks with a pout.

"No, go ahead, order, and eat. I don't know how long it will take us to get the footage," Shane says.

"You mean a quickie," Heath quips with a smirk before debarking off the train.

Nora looks at us both, while Shane and I both shake our heads in disbelief.

"Does he have a filter?" Shane asks me.

"None," I reply.

We all walk up the stairs to the station parting ways as Nora and Heath head out to the diner, while Shane and I head to the security office.

As soon as we walk in, the officer in the room hands Shane a thumb drive. "Here you go, Detective, already have it ready for you today."

"Thanks, I appreciate it."

Shane pockets the thumb drive, and we walk out of the station and to the car. Once we are both in, Shane pulls my head to him and slams his lips on mine. I melt under his kiss, pushing my chest out, needing him to touch me.

He pulls back from the kiss, both of us breathing hard. His eyes are dark blue, full of need and lust. Without saying a word, he puts the car in reverse, backs out of the space, and drives. He reaches his hand over and places it on my thigh. I instinctively open my legs wider, needing him to touch me.

He glides his hand up, just staying out of reach of where I want him. He squeezes my thigh as I notice he is pulling into my hotel parking lot.

He parks the car, turns to me, and says, "I need you, love. I need to be buried inside you."

"Yes," I whisper because I need that too.

We make our way to my room, and as soon as the door closes, he pushes me up against the door, claiming my lips possessively, and I allow him. I didn't realize we were both unbuttoning each other's shirts until we were shrugging out of them. He undoes his pants and takes them off as I do the same with mine.

Once we are both naked, I drop to my knees, needing to taste him. I lick the precum from his slit and swirl my tongue around his head. He tastes amazing, and I can't help the moan that leaves me. I lick his shaft from his base to his head, before wrapping my hand around the bottom and stroking him up as I place my mouth over his cock and suck him in.

I hear his sharp intake of breath and look up at him.

"Oh, fuck, that feels so good, love. I've imagined this a thousand times, and the real thing is so much better," he tells me, and I can't help the pride that swells up inside me.

I show him just what his words mean to me, and I continue sucking and licking his cock.

"I'm close, baby, and I don't want to come in your mouth, I want to be in your pussy," he tells me.

I allow his cock to pop out of my mouth like a blow-pop lollipop. He helps me up off the floor and leads me to the bed as he kisses my lips, our tongues battling again, showing how much we both need and want each other.

He lays me on the bed, stepping between my legs, and slowly entering me. The stretch is both painful and pleasurable. Once he's fully in, he begins to thrust in me, and I move my hips to match his thrusts with my own.

"Oh, God," I call out.

"Fuck," he says at the same time.

We are both wanting to take our time and yet hurry it up, needing to find our releases.

He leans down and captures my mouth again in a sweet kiss, and in this moment, I know I have given this man my heart and soul. I deepen the kiss, pouring every ounce of what I feel for this man but cannot say aloud, into this kiss, hoping he understands.

We both come together, prolonging the orgasm as we both try to catch our breaths.

"Wow," he says. "I think that was better than this morning's earlier session."

"I agree," I say with a giggle and a smile, "But we should get dressed and meet up with Heath and Nora, before we don't hear the end of it," I add.

"I know you are right, but would it be wrong if I said I just wanted to spend the day curled up with you?" he asks.

"No, it wouldn't be. I want that too, but work must come first."

"He sighs and says, "You're right. Come, let's get dressed."

He helps me up, and I walk into the bathroom to clean up, before putting my clothes back on and fixing my hair.

Shane and I get to the diner just as the waitress is serving Heath and Nora their breakfasts. We place our order with her, and she walks away.

A thought hits me, and I say, "I've had a thought, we need to go back to Maine."

"What?" Shane asks.

"Why?" Heath asks at the same time.

I hold my hand up. "First, we need some new clothes, but second, and most importantly, we need to see if we can get security footage of who boarded the train there this morning and see if we can possibly catch the killer from that," I tell the table.

"Good point," Shane says.

"We've been looking at security footage of those here, debarking, but never have we considered when they get onboard," I elaborate.

"That's true, and I do need to change out my outfits," Heath says.

"When will you go back?" Shane asks.

"We can all go right after you complete the notifications. The coroner said he should have their personal belongings in a couple of hours. I'm sure she has a purse, and he has a wallet, so once you have those and make the notifications to the next of kins, we can make the four-hour drive back to Largo this evening. We also need to check in with our team and see how they are really doing with finding our friend," I say softly, as the waitress brings Shane and I's food.

"We? As in all of us?" Shane asks.

"Yes," I say, taking a bite of my eggs.

"We will need to clear it with the Commander, but okay," he says with a smile.

"How long will we be staying, Hunnybun?" Heath asks.

"Well, today is Monday, but it will depend on how much security footage we can get. If they still have from the very first murder to the latest, I think that would be better for our case," I tell them all and watch everyone's head nod.

"Will it at least be overnight?"

"Definitely. Shane and Nora, you are more than welcome to come stay at my place," I say with a giggle before continuing, "I think Heath will be getting kinky and making up for the last two weeks."

"I am not ashamed to admit, I am a needy hussy," he says, taking a bite of his sausage link.

I burst out laughing, I can't help myself, but keep my remark about small things in my head.

"If you don't mind, I think I'll stay here and spend time watching the security footage from today, also I may have a little lead on Courtney," Nora says.

Shane looks at her, and she says, "Don't worry, I'm not getting my hopes up, but someone said they think they may have seen her down on the train platform a few times, so I want to check out the footage and see if they are right," she tells Shane, and he nods.

"Whose Courtney?" I ask, completely lost.

"Courtney is my best friend, and she was my husband's secretary."

Both Heath and I gasp.

"I'm sorry, but husband? Girl, you didn't tell me you were married," Heath says.

"Was. I'm a widow for the last six and a half months," Nora says.

"Oh, sweetie, I'm sorry. What happened?" Heath asks.

"They were on a train, coming back from a conference, and the working theory is a group or gang must have been harassing them or trying to rob them. Ben was stabbed multiple times, presumably to protect Courtney. He was killed, and she disappeared. There were no witnesses as to what happened, and I've been searching for her ever since," Nora says, teary-eyed.

"Oh, sweetie," Heath says, pulling her into his side for a hug. "We understand what it's like to lose your best friend and not know what happened. We are also going through that. Kim is my bitch, and I'm completely lost without her. Even though it helps to have something else to focus on, all we keep hoping for is they walk back into our lives, and they are okay."

She nods her head as he holds her.

"If you need any help from us, please don't hesitate to ask. We will try to help in any way we can," I say, reaching my hand across the table, and she accepts it, giving it a little squeeze.

"Thank you, I appreciate it, but I'm not sure what more can be done. I've been monitoring her bank accounts, and there have been no movements. If she is out there, I don't know how she is surviving, but if someone has her, I can't even fathom who, and that makes my heart hurt for what she had possibly been going through for the last six months," Nora says, as she allows the tears to fall.

My heart hurts for her because we know exactly how she feels. It hurts my heart to think what Kim could be going through.

Chapter Sixteen

SHANE

My heart breaks for what Nora is going through, and the fact that Heath and Mya can relate with their friend missing as well, but I also can't lie, my heart is soaring with the revelation that Mya wants me to come to Maine with her.

I thought she wanted to leave and maybe regretted the time we spent together, but I do agree with her idea of getting the security footage from the Maine train station and comparing it to the footage we have here.

Once Nora calms down and washes her face, I pay for everyone's breakfast as we all head back to the precinct to brief Commander Doyle.

Mya calls her boss and talks with him about her theory, and he agrees to it, also letting her know, there is no news on Kim.

When we walk into the precinct, Commander Doyle is waiting for us. We all walk into the conference room and begin to debrief him.

He rubs his hands down his face and says, "I'm going to need to let the public know that we have brought in the FBI with this latest murder, otherwise, they may think we aren't taking this seriously enough."

"I agree," Mya tells him. "Hopefully, we will get something off the security footage in Largo that will help us."

"Sir, I'd like to go with the Agents back to Largo. I'm hoping we can not only get this morning's footage, but of the last three murders."

"Fine. Riley, will you be going as well?" he asks her.

"No, Sir, I'll be staying here and going back through our footage as well as the files, that way if anyone has any questions, I'm here with answers," she tells him, and he seems pleased with that.

"What about the two Directors at Boston General?" he asks.

"They both seemed to have disappeared for the moment, but I'm sure they will turn up. Neither one can afford to lose their jobs at the moment, though if they are involved in the thefts of the medication, then they lose everything anyways," Mya tells him. "I will continue to monitor their accounts," she adds.

This seems to placate the Commander, and he nods.

"Fine, sounds like we are doing everything we can at the moment. I will put out the information on them, asking for the public's help in locating them as they may have viable information to the case, but I will ensure to emphasize they are not persons of interest in these cases."

"That's perfect," Mya tells him with a smile, and the man actually smiles back at her.

I don't think I have ever seen the Commander smile before, to be honest.

"What?" he asks, looking over at me.

"Nothing, Sir," I say, not wanting to irritate or offend him before I leave with Mya.

My phone rings, and it's Max.

"Max, do you have the identification of the victims?" I ask.

"I do. You are more than welcome to come down and get them. I will be performing the autopsy on both victims soon. We still have not received the toxicology reports on our last two victims yet."

"That's fine. I don't think they will say anything much different than the others," I tell him before adding, **"I'll be down there shortly to pick up the items."**

I hang up the phone and look at the Commander, "Max has found the victims identification."

"Good, go pick it up and make the notifications. We need to find the person responsible for these murders as soon as possible. Hopefully Maine can shed some light for us," he says before walking out of the conference room.

"Come on, Nora, let's do this," I say as we both stand up.

"Let us know if you need any help with next of kin details," Mya says.

"I will definitely call you when we have the names, so we don't have to return until after the notifications have been completed," I tell her with a smile, and she smiles back.

"I'd say get a room, but you two have already done that," Heath pipes in.

I watch as Mya's face turns red and love it when she blushes.

Nora and I walk out of the conference room, going straight for the front doors.

When we get in the car, Nora asks, "Is this serious?"

I look over at her questioningly.

"Are you and Mya serious, or is this a fling?"

I smile, "This is serious. I have never felt like this with anyone. She makes my world brighter than I ever thought it could be. I know it seems sudden, but I can't imagine life without her in it," I tell her honestly.

"Does she feel the same way?"

"I think so, but we haven't really had a chance to have that conversation yet," I tell her.

"Then I am very happy for you both," she says with a smile, but it doesn't reach her eyes, and I wonder if it's because she's thinking about her husband or her best friend.

We get to the morgue, and Max points to the items on the counter. I hand Nora the female's purse, while I open the man's wallet. I locate his driver's license, telling me his name is Donovan Whister. I also find a Gentleman's Club card in his wallet with five hundred in cash.

Nora holds up the female's ID, showing me her name is Jennifer Carey, both are from New York.

We gather up the items, putting them into evidence bags. I will need to call New York once we have the next of kin information and let them make the notifications.

"Thanks, Max," I tell him, but he just waves.

We get back to the precinct, and I pass both names of the victims to Mya, who looks up their next of kin information.

"As expected, Mr. Whistler is married to Bernice, has three kids, all in college at NYU, and he's the CEO at Pharmtech in New York, and his address is 400 Broadlear Dr, PH 2, in New York," she says, and I jot the information down.

"Jennifer Carey, also married. Her husband's name is Jonathan, they have no kids, and she works as a secretary at Pharmtech in New York. Her address is 95 Hawkins Rd, Lot 41, in Wap Falls, NY."

I leave the conference room to make some calls. It takes me half an hour to get someone to do both notifications to the next of kin. When I walk back into the conference room, I see Heath sleeping in a chair, and Mya on her laptop.

"Shall we go back to your hotel so you can grab your things and check out?"

"Sure, but you are going to need to pack a bag as well, right?" she asks.

"Yes, ma'am, but we can stop by my place after we take care of your things," I tell her softly before adding, "Do you want to wake sleeping beauty, or should I?"

She giggles, and Heath says, "I'm not sleeping hoes, but can we get food before we hit the road? I am hungry again."

Mya and I both can't help the laughs that escape us.

"Let's go, bottomless pit," Mya jokes.

Heath stands up, and I help Mya from her seat. She packs up her laptop and zips the bag just as Nora walks in.

"Are you all leaving already?" she asks softly.

"Yes, but we will be back, so keep my seat warm for me," Heath says before hugging her.

Mya also hugs Nora, "Remember if you need anything, just call us, we should be back in a couple of days."

Nora nods as she pulls away from the hug.

"I'll call you once we have the footage," I tell her, and she nods.

I follow Heath and Mya out of the conference room and find the Commander waiting for us. "Before you go, I received a call from the missing persons division, seems Mr. Arnold Fischer reported his wife,

Gretchen, missing. Said she never came home last night, and he was told she left the office yesterday afternoon."

"Is she missing, or did she run?" Mya asks.

"Right now, we will treat it as a missing case, and I will reiterate that in my press conference this afternoon," he tells us, and we all nod.

"We should be back in a couple of days, hopefully with some new leads or news," I tell him, and he nods.

"Be safe, all of you," he tells us before walking away.

We continue out of the precinct, getting in the car, and I drive them both to the hotel. Once they pack their belongings and check out, they get in their car and follow me to my house so I can pack a bag before I ride with them.

I'm excited to be going to Maine with Mya, but I try not to let the giddiness show.

Once I'm packed and the house is locked up, we stop to get something to eat. Since Heath was hungry, we allowed him to choose what he wanted to eat, and he chose sandwiches. I directed Mya to the best sandwich shop in Boston. In my opinion, they have a perfect Philly cheesesteak.

We walk in, and the owner, Mr. Lionel, greets me by name, "Hey Shane, it's been a while."

He's an older, Italian, gentleman in his 60's, but you would never know it by the way he still moves around. The friendliest man I have ever met and knows all his customers by name and order.

"Hey, Mr. Lionel. Yeah, things have been crazy busy lately," I tell him.

"You bring me two newbies?" he calls out.

"I did. Meet Mya and Heath, they are from Maine," I tell him.

"Ahh, I love new people," he says as he walks around the counter. "You are a very tall, young man, I bet you eat a lot," he tells Heath and Mya giggles.

"Yes, Sir, I do," Heath replies, not ashamed to admit it.

"Do you cook?" he asks him.

"No, Sir," Heath responds.

"Learn to cook, you make a man very happy when you fill his belly right," Mr. Lionel says.

I watch as Heath blushes.

He looks over at Mya, "Ahh, pretty one. You are strong and tough," he says, looking at her, then he looks up at me and nods. "You will make my Shane happy, and he will make you happy. It's a perfect union," he tells us, taking both of our hands and clasping them together. "This is real love," he says, and I watch as Mya's face turns crimson.

"Yes, yes, I can see these things," he tells us, going back around the counter, "Go take a seat, and I'll bring you each something special," he tells us.

I find us a table in the corner.

"He is interesting," Mya whispers.

"Yes, he is, but he is never wrong," I whisper back to her.

Mr. Lionel brings out three footlong Philly cheesesteak sandwiches and a bag full of fries, placing them on the table in front of each of us.

"Here you go, eat now, you have a long drive ahead of you," he says.

Sometimes, I think the man has psychic abilities. "Thank you, Mr. Lionel, this looks wonderful as usual," I tell him.

He's watching Mya as she takes a bite of the sandwich and moans. "This is amazing. Thank you so much."

Mr. Lionel smiles, "I knew you'd like it," he says as he winks at me.

"This is really good, thank you," Heath says.

"How you know? You inhaled half the sandwich already. Did you even taste it?" Mr. Lionel asks, and Mya busts out laughing as I chuckle.

Heath looks at Mr. Lionel and says with a straight face, "Mr. Lionel, if it wasn't good, it wouldn't go in my mouth. I can be very picky about things like that."

Mr. Lionel laughs. "Oh, you are going to make a wonderful wife one day, my boy," he tells him as he pats him on the shoulder and walks away, still chuckling.

We continue eating, with Heath being the first one finished. He's looking at the other half of Mya's sandwich with longing, and she passes it over to him.

"Here, you know I can't eat anything this massive," she says.

"Do you need me to teach you, or is he just that small?" Heath asks before taking a bite out of the sandwich.

I choke, and Mya says, "That," pointing at my lower area, "Is not your concern," she starts to say, but I interrupt.

"She definitely doesn't need any lessons in that department," I say and watch as Mya blushes again.

"Oh, you are holding out on the deets," Heath says, now looking interested and intrigued.

Mya groans before saying, "We are not discussing this. Eat your sandwich."

Heath chuckles but picks up the sandwich and continues eating.

We finish eating our meal and say good-bye to Mr. Lionel before getting in the car and starting the drive to Maine.

Chapter Seventeen

MYA

It's been two hours since we left Boston, and I'm driving, while Shane sits up front with me and Heath sleeps in the back. I love my friend, but sometimes he can be so embarrassing, I think to myself as I shake my head, remembering the comment he said about Shane.

I did love that Shane let me and Heath know he had no problems with how I performed on him this morning. Thinking about it, I can't help the blush that creeps up.

"What is it, love?" Shane asks.

"I'm just remembering what Heath said at the sandwich shop. I'm sorry about that. I love him, but sometimes he has no filter," I tell Shane, and he laughs.

"I know, and there is no reason to be embarrassed. After two weeks around him, I've gotten used to his unfilterness," Shane responds.

"Don't you mean my honesty?" Heath says, though his eyes are still closed.

"No," I say.

He chuckles. "Well at least you love me. I know how hard that is for you to say," he says.

"Asshole," I mutter, and Heath laughs out loud.

Two hours later, we finally pull up to the office building, and I park the car. We all grab our bags out of the trunk, and I lead Shane to my car to store our stuff before we walk into the building, taking the elevator up to the fourth floor.

I'm a little nervous about how the team will treat Shane, but we walk off the elevator and into our suite. I lay my laptop bag on my desk, and we all walk into the conference room. Eric, Michelle, Frankie, and Declan are all in there, using the whiteboard, but I notice a lot of things have been crossed off.

"Hey," I say. "Eric, this is Detective Shane Maguire, Shane, this is our boss, Special Agent Eric Chandler," I say, introducing them.

"Detective, nice to meet you. I have heard good things about your Division," Eric tells him as they shake hands.

"Thank you, Sir. I'll pass that down to my Commander," Shane responds.

"This is Eric's wife, Michelle, she's also our State Medical Examiner, and these two are Agent Frankie Mathis and Agent Declan Carr," I finish with the introductions of the team.

Shane nods to everyone, shaking their hands.

"Here," Eric says, handing me several thumb drives.

"Are these the security footage from the train station?" I ask.

"Yes, I figured you could use these quickly," he tells us.

"Thank you. Any new leads?" I ask, looking at the whiteboard.

"No," Michelle says softly.

I walk over and squeeze her hand. "What help do you all need?" I ask.

"We've finished going through all the past case files, checked on all the convicted, their families, and associates. We found nothing," Frankie says.

Michelle tears up, and Eric pulls her close. "We are not giving up on finding her, and I know wherever she is, she is fighting to get back to us," Eric says, and I nod in agreement.

"As hard as this is to say, I think everyone needs to go home and decompress for the night," I hold up my hand because I know Declan is getting ready to argue with me.

"Listen, I'm not saying don't care, I'm saying walk away tonight, get a good meal, watch some TV, go to the gym, or whatever it is you like to do normally, then get a good night's sleep. None of you look like you've slept in two weeks. When you take care of yourself, things seem clearer. Then come back refreshed, and maybe something you haven't thought of will come to mind. As long as we all keep going around in circles nothing will get accomplished. Kim needs us all at our best, and right now, no one is at their best," I tell them all, but looking pointedly at Declan, who looks worse than everyone else.

Eric nods.

"How about we all go get something to eat together, Heath and I can catch you up on the Train Killer, everyone can eat, then go home and do whatever relaxes you before you go to sleep," I tell them.

"Okay," Michelle says, softly. "You are right, we can't keep going in circles, we need something new or fresh eyes."

I look over at Frankie, he nods, then I look at Declan, he takes a deep sigh, then nods in agreement.

"I'm going to call Chris and see if he is available to come," Heath says, stepping out to call Chris.

Everyone shuts off their computers, turning off the lights as we walk out. I quickly grab my laptop case, and shut the door behind me, while Eric locks it.

"Where shall we go to eat?" I ask the group when the elevator doors open.

"Let's go to the Italian place down the road," Declan suggests, and it makes me happy to see he is taking what I said to heart.

"That sounds perfect," Michelle says as we get off the elevator and we walk down the sidewalk to the restaurant.

I watch as Heath sends Chris a text telling him where to meet us.

Eric goes in first to get us a table, and we wait until he comes out to tell us they have one available that will accommodate us.

We all make our way inside and follow the hostess to a table in the back. A few minutes after we sit down, Chris comes in and makes his way to our table.

"Hey, everyone," Chris says, taking a seat next to Heath. "Hey babe, missed you," he whispers to him.

"Missed you too," Heath says, smiling big at Chris.

Heath had already ordered Chris a drink, so the waitress went around the table taking our orders.

Shane and I both order the lasagna meal, once orders are taken, conversation flows freely, and there is no discussion about work, or Kim, though we can all feel her absence around the table. I do give credit to everyone, they are at least trying.

Once dinner is done, everyone heads back to the parking lot at work and gets in their vehicles, waving good night to each other.

I drive us to my place, and I'm a bit nervous taking Shane to my apartment. It isn't much, but it's home for when I'm there.

"Dinner was great," Shane says.

"It was, and I'm glad most everyone allowed themselves to relax," I tell him as we pull into my complex.

I park the car, and we both exit it, going to the trunk to get our bags.

"They all were really trying, though I have to ask, is Declan and Kim in a relationship?"

"That is a good question. I think they are, though neither one has ever admitted to it, and I'm wondering if they are taking a page out of Michelle and Eric's book," I tell him, leading him up the walkway to my door.

"Huh?" he asks, and I know he is confused.

"I'll explain inside," I tell him as I place the key in the door, unlocking it, and turning the knob to open.

We walk inside, and I drop my keys and purse on the console table, before walking over to the thermostat and dropping the temperature. Now that I am home, I want to be comfortable, but there is no reason to run it if I'm not there.

I take my bag to the bedroom, open it up, and put all the clothes in the laundry hamper. Shane follows me into the bedroom, and I tell him, "You can put your bag over there if you want," as I grab the hamper and walk to the washing machine down the hall. I get the laundry started, and then ask him, "Want some coffee?"

"Sure, coffee sounds good," he calls back.

I make my way to the kitchen and start a pot of coffee, and Shane walks in.

"You have a nice place," he tells me.

"Thanks, it's not much, but it's enough for me. The open floor plan, kitchen, eat-in kitchen or dining room, whichever you prefer, then the living room, two bedrooms, two bathrooms. I do like the fact that each bedroom has its own bathroom. Out back, through the door, there is a nice little patio, so when I am home and have time, I have a place to sit outside."

"It's cute. I wouldn't expect anything more for you," he tells me, pulling me into his arms and giving me a soft kiss.

When he pulls back, he asks, "Do you want to go through the security footage tonight?"

"No. I meant what I said to the team, we should all do something to clear our minds of cases. I suggest we watch a movie together, what do you think?" I ask him.

"I like that idea," he says with a smile.

"Good, you go stream through and see what interests you and I'll get our coffees," I tell him.

He kisses my lips one more time before walking into the living room, sitting on the couch, and grabbing the remote.

I take down two coffee cups from the cupboard and pour our coffee. I make mine just how I like with sugar and creamer, and I know Shane takes his black.

I take the cups to the living room, where Shane is waiting for me, and pass him his before sitting down next to him.

"What did you decide?" I ask.

"I figured a comedy was in order, so how about the greatest movie of all time, 'Tommy Boy'?" he asks.

"I have not seen that movie in ages, that's perfect," I tell him.

He hits start, and I move in between his legs so I can lay my head on his chest. I don't know when I fell asleep, one minute I was laughing, and the next, I could feel Shane picking me up and carrying me to bed.

He helps me get undressed, but as soon as we are cuddled up together under the covers, I'm out, and I don't wake again until my alarm goes off at seven am.

I roll over and turn it off, stretching, and then I hear Shane ask, "Did you sleep well last night?"

"I did? Did you?" I ask, nervous if he didn't.

"With you in my arms, I can sleep like the dead. Prior to you, I never really felt like I slept," he tells me honestly, and I can't help the smile that forms on my face.

"Go take a shower, I'll make the coffee this morning," Shane tells me, and I lean over to give him a good morning kiss, which he deepens, then breaks off. "Go, or neither one of us is getting any work done today."

I laugh because he is probably right. I start the shower while he starts the coffee. I quickly wash up, get out, and dry off. I walk into my closet, and because I will be working from home, I opt to wear a pair of jeans and a T-shirt.

I towel dry my wet hair, then run a comb through it, deciding to leave it down today to air dry instead of putting it up.

I walk out into the kitchen. "Shane, you can get in the shower now before we start," I say as I grab my coffee cup Shane made off the counter and take a sip. "Wow," I say, loving the taste.

"Wow, is right. You look hot," Shane says, causing me to turn around. "I didn't realize your hair is so long. It's beautiful, and you definitely know how to rock some jeans."

I giggle, this man sure knows how to make me feel special and hot.

"Go get in the shower, Heath should be here soon," I tell him with a smile.

"Yeah, work, right," he says, sounding very distracted, and I love that I can do that to him.

I don't know what our future holds with him in Boston and me here, but I want this, and I know there has to be a way for us to make it all work, that is if he wants to, I think to myself.

I hear a knock on the door, and I know it's Heath, so I walk over and answer, allowing him to come in.

"Oh, do you have one of those for me?" he asks, though he should know better.

"You know where it's at," I tell him, walking over to the dining room table.

"You left your hair down today, I like it. You should do that more often," Heath tells me.

"No, it would only get in the way at work," I tell him honestly as I insert a thumb drive.

"Where is McHotty? Did you wear him out, that he has to sleep longer?" Heath asks.

"No, we both slept last night, and he is currently in the shower," I tell him.

"So, you didn't christen the house or your bed?" he asks, shocked.

"No, we watched a movie, and I fell asleep."

"Boring," he says, feigning a yawn. "I got mine last night."

"That I had no doubt about," I tell him with a chuckle.

Chapter Eighteen

SHANE

I walk out of the bedroom and hear voices, letting me know Heath is here. I opted to wear jeans and a T-shirt, just as Mya had. Her home is small, not much space, but it's cozy and homey. I really like it. It suits her.

I walk into the kitchen, refilling my coffee cup, before I walk over to the table. "Good morning, Heath," I say as I take a sip.

"Oh, McHotty, you know how to rock jeans too, damn you both are so hot, you are going to make beautiful babies, and I call dibs on being their Fairy Godfather," he says happily with a smile.

I choke on my coffee, definitely not expecting that, though the thought of seeing Mya's belly swollen with my children, calms me like the idea has never done before.

"Heath, stop that," Mya says, blushing again.

I opt for a safer topic. "Are you going to play that on the TV where we can all see it?"

"Yes, but right now, I'm looking to make sure I get the thumb drives in the right order that we need," she tells me.

I nod and walk into the living room, taking a seat on the couch.

"Okay, got it," she calls out, and I turn the TV on and get it set to the right HDMI.

Mya connects her laptop, then presses play so we can watch.

"Okay, here is the first couple, definitely not paying attention to anyone around them," Mya says, taking a seat next to me.

She has a notebook and pen on the coffee table that she picks up to jot notes or observations.

"Wait, is that Rayeanne in the ticket line?" Heath asks.

"Rayeanne Burton, the missing girl that's been all over the news in Boston?" I ask.

"Yes. Her grandfather is a homicide detective in Chatam County. According to her friend, she was on her way to New York to visit NYU, but the last place her phone pinged was in Boston. No one has seen her since she boarded the train," Mya tells me.

"Do you know her grandfather?" I ask.

"Yes. Our last serial killer killed two women from his county," Heath responds.

"Wow. Okay, so we have two issues going on in this video," I say.

"Exactly, but I have watched your videos in Boston, and never once did I see her or someone dressed like her get off the train in Boston," Mya says.

"So how did she disappear?" I mumble, but Mya hears me.

"That is the million-dollar question, almost like Courtney," she says, and I nod.

We continue to watch the video of the victims making out before the platform opens for boarding.

"Well, they sure were not discreet about their affair outside of Boston," I say.

"No, it doesn't seem that way," Mya mutters in disgust.

We watch as the victims stand in line at the business car, still making out, but no one seems to be paying them special attention.

The conductors come out, checking tickets and allowing everyone to board. When the victims get to the conductor, he is looking the female up and down. It looks like he asks her a question, but she shakes her head and cozies back up to the male. When they board, the conductor looks upset.

"Does that man look upset to you?" I ask the other two, and both agree.

Mya jots down to find out his name and see if he is also on the other three trains.

"There's Rayeanne," Heath exclaims, and we watch her run up to the train in economy, passing him her ticket before getting on board.

"So, she did get on the train," Mya says.

"Should we tell Detective Burton?" Heath asks.

"I'm sure he already knows and already has a copy of this security footage. We wouldn't be telling him anything new," Mya says, and Heath concedes she's probably right.

We watch as the conductors make the last call before getting on the train. We watch the train pull away.

"Did you by chance, bring the thumb drives from Boston?" Mya asks me.

"I did," I tell her, getting up and retrieving them from my bag.

I bring them to the living room and pass them over to her.

"Perfect. Thank you," she says with a smile.

"Anytime," I say as I lean down to kiss her, before taking a seat.

"Okay, first, I want us to rewatch the first one, look for anything out of the ordinary, then we will watch when the train gets to Boston and see what doesn't fit," Mya says, and both Heath and I nod.

We watch the first victims, and I'm trying to catch anything out of the ordinary, but nothing jumps out at me, except the victims making out. Then Mya places the Boston drive in, and we watch that.

"Wait," she says, pausing the footage.

"What is it?" I ask.

"How long is the stop normally in Boston, before the train leaves for New York?" she asks.

"About forty-five minutes," I say.

"If someone has a ticket to New York, they don't have to get off the train if they don't want to, correct?"

"That is true," I say, still trying to catch up to where she is going with this.

"What do the conductors do during this stop? Shouldn't they be making sure that the passengers still on the train are actually going to New York?"

"Yes," I say, still a little slow.

"So what were they doing for thirty minutes before the bodies were found and the police were alerted? Who told the passengers to disembark from the train, and where would they go to catch one to New York? Also, who would have told the passengers that got off for a break about the new train? I'm sure someone asked about their bags and such," Mya states.

"Wow, you are brilliant. None of those questions ever crossed my mind. But we know the third and fourth couple victims were found by other passengers, only the first two were found by conductors," I tell her.

"So let's time the second train," she says as she puts the thumb drive in, and we watch.

Again, this couple is also making out for the world to see. We watch as they board business class with the same conductor as before. Again, he interacts with the female, and we watch as she shakes her head before getting on the train, with the man saying something to the conductor before he gets on behind the female.

"We definitely need to find out who he is," I say.

We watch the train leave, then change to the next thumb drive, where they arrive in Boston. Again, it's thirty minutes before anyone notices and reports.

We watch the final two days, and the same conductor is onboarding the business car and says something to the females, who all shake their heads no.

"I wonder what he asked them?" I say aloud.

"Me too," Mya says.

"Looks like we may have our suspect," I add.

"I agree. I think you and I should take the train back to Boston tomorrow and meet this conductor," Mya says, then looks over at Heath, "Are you okay to drive to Boston, or would you prefer to take the train as well?"

"I think we should all take the train. You too can take business class, and I'll take economy class, see if the conductor can recall anything about Rayeanne," he says.

"I like that. Okay, looks like we are taking an army train tomorrow morning. Let me call Eric and tell him our plans and what we may have found," Mya says, getting up from the couch and grabbing her phone.

In the morning, we all arrive early at the Largo Amtrak station. Mya already purchased the tickets with approval from Eric and Commander Doyle. When I called him, explaining what we found and suspected, he was onboard with the idea and wished us luck. All we need to do is go in and take a seat.

"Okay, Heath, Shane, and I will make out like the other victims, try to do the same things they did," Mya tells him.

"You just want a reason to make out," Heath says, laughing, and I can't say he's wrong, at least on my end. I watch as Mya blushes, and I think it's true for her as well.

"Just observe and let me know if you see anything off," Mya tells him.

"Those are off," he says, pointing to someone's pajamas. "That style went out in the ninety's for persnickety sake, why are people so keen to bring that God awful shit back?" he says, and I can't help but laugh, as we leave him to judge what people are wearing this early in the morning.

Both Mya and I are dressed in our business work attire. We start by sitting in the same vicinity as all the victims did and begin to make out.

God, I could kiss this woman all day and night. Nothing, and I mean nothing, feels or tastes better than her. My hand snakes up her shirt to cup her breast, and I hear her moan as I tease her nipple.

I forget we are in a train station until I hear the boarding call.

"Damn, baby, I'm sorry. I forgot where we were," I tell her softly as I try to get my breathing, and hard-on under control.

"I know, me too," she whispers back, taking deep breaths to also get her breathing under control.

We stand up together and grab our bags, walking toward the platform and our car. We stand in line, and I nibble on her ear, and neck and she giggles.

We get to the conductor, and it's the same man from the videos.

"Hello folks, I need to see your tickets, please," he says, looking Mya up and down as I pass the phone with the tickets to him to scan.

"My name is Cavanaugh, but you can call me Casanova, pretty lady," he tells Mya, and I want to punch him.

"Interesting name," she says, playing along.

"Have you ever wanted a duo?" he asks, and she shakes her head.

"No, one is more than enough for me," she says, siding up to me.

"Let me know if you change your mind. I promise it's an experience you will never forget," he says with a wink.

"I'm sure I won't," she says, boarding.

I look at him and say with a growl in my voice, "Next time, you might want to ask me if I want you to join in before you ask my woman."

I get on the train behind Mya, and we look for our seats.

I let her sit by the window, and I take the aisle. If given the opportunity, I think I want to trip that fucker before I arrest him.

"Calm down," Mya whispers.

I kiss her lips, and that does calm me for now.

Chapter Nineteen

MYA

I pull back from the kiss with Shane, I can tell he's riled up by what Cavanaugh, AKA Cassanova, insinuated. *I wonder if that's the same offer he gave to the other women,* I think to myself.

I don't have time to dwell on it too much as the man in question boards the car and walks the aisle. Once he sees me, he winks, and I have to hold Shane's hand to keep him from jumping up and punching the man.

"Okay, ladies and gentlemen, the train will be departing in a few short minutes. Please ensure all your items are put away. The cafe will open once the train is in full motion. Don't worry, I will let you all know when that time is. For now, sit back and enjoy the seats or whatever you prefer to ride on," he says with a smirk, and it makes my skin crawl, but it is telling that he may have witnessed the last couple.

He walks back down the aisle and out of the car, presumably to the next one.

"He is definitely someone who needs to be questioned, no matter what," Shane says.

"I agree. He obviously saw that couple having sex, so makes me wonder what else he may have seen," I reply quietly to him.

He nods but says nothing more. I close my eyes and lay my head on Shane's shoulder. He grabs my hand, holds it, and allows me to sleep for a little bit.

I wake to the smell of coffee, not knowing how long I had been out. "Is that coffee?" I ask.

Shane chuckles and says, "Yes. Heath brought us both a cup since he knew I wouldn't leave you while you were sleeping."

"Oh, that was so sweet of him," I say, taking my cup from him. "Thank you," I tell him before asking, "How long was I out?"

"Forty-five minutes," he tells me.

"Not too bad then," I say, and he chuckles while we both drink our coffee.

"Have you seen the conductor?"

"The last time he came through, was to tell everyone the cafe was open, then he went back through that door, and I haven't seen him since," Shane tells me.

"Interesting, I wonder where he is?"

"The question is, how long will we have to wait for him to come back to the car once we reach Boston?"

"That's a good point," I say, sipping on my coffee, while wondering where the conductor would go on the train.

"We have about an hour before we pull into Boston, do you want to take a walk to the cafe for more coffee? Gives us a chance to check things out," Shane asks, with a shrug, and I can't help the giggle that escapes me. The man is so damn cute.

"Yes, let's do that because I'm curious where he could be spending his time. Plus, I need more coffee," I tell him, and this time he laughs.

We get up from our seats, and he allows me to walk in front of him. My phone vibrates, and I look down to see a text from Heath,

> Bitch, you awake yet?

I text him back.

> **Yes. Going to the cafe for more coffee and to look around. Want to join us?**

> Hell yes. I'm bored, and these people aren't chatty.

I chuckle, and Shane looks at me quizzically.

"Heath is bored," I tell him, and he nods in understanding.

We walk through the car door and into the next car. I look around at the people on their laptops, phones, or tablets. Some, though not many, are sleeping, but the majority seems to be working on something in this car. Shane and I continue forward until we come to the cafe car. There is a small line, so I browse the menu, while we wait.

Heath comes in a few minutes after us and steps in line behind us.

"Oh my God, this train ride is so boring."

"What did you think it would be like?" I ask curiously because I never considered what being on the train could be like.

"I don't know, people wanting to get to know people, have some laughs, but I am literally in a car full of sleeping duds. I tried to engage one lady into a conversation, and she threatened to call the police and have me banned," he says, laughing.

"Did she give a reason?" I ask.

"I was being too nosey, so I must be up to no good," he says, rolling his eyes, and I have to laugh at that statement.

"Well, you can be a little more inquisitive than most people," I tell him.

"I like conversation. I like getting to know people. Is that so wrong?" he asks, pouting.

"No, sweetie, it's not wrong, you just have to know your crowd, and obviously that isn't it," I tell him as I give him a sad face.

"Right. So, tell me about the conductor," he says, getting into work mode.

"Let's grab coffee and a sandwich, then we can sit down and chat. In fact, I'll get the orders, and you guys go find us a table out of the way," I tell both of them just as the lady calls next, and that's us.

I step up to the counter, ordering all of us a coffee and breakfast sandwich. The lady hands me my order, and I thank her, before carrying everything over to the table that the men found. I pass everything out and then take a seat.

I take a bite of my sandwich and take a sip of my coffee, as Shane explains everything that's happened with the conductor so far.

"Whoo, the man seriously asked for a threesome?" Heath questions.

"Pretty much, yep," I say before taking a sip of my coffee, then continue, "Makes me wonder if that's exactly what he said to all the other women."

"I'm just floored he was awake to come on board," Heath says.

"Oh, I had a few words with him before I boarded," Shane says, but I interrupt.

"Though I don't think he took the hint, by the remark he made when he was briefing us before the train started to move." I tell Heath about the comment of riding on the seat or wherever and the smirk.

"Interesting. So, the man definitely saw something. Did he ever get interviewed last time?" Heath asks.

"I don't know, and we don't have that file with us, since the murders just happened a couple of days ago," Shane says, but I make a mental note to check when we get back to the precinct.

"My question is, where has he been all this time? Shane says he hasn't been back in the car since announcing the cafe was open?"

"Maybe the conductors get their own private cars," Heath says with a shrug.

"Huh?" I ask.

"There are private cars on the train. They cost a pretty penny, but you essentially get your own room where you can sleep, change, and you have your own bathroom," he informs me.

"How did I not know this?" I ask, flabbergasted.

"You don't do enough research," Heath says jokingly. However, in this case, he is right.

"I wonder if we can have a look at these private cars?" I muse.

"I'll text Nora and see if she can get us a search warrant in case they don't allow us access," Shane says, grabbing his phone and shooting off a text.

A few seconds later, I hear a ping. "She's on it," Shane says, reading the text. "She'll meet us at the station when we arrive."

"Will she be able to find a judge to sign off on it this early in the morning?" I ask.

"Nora will find the judge, don't worry," Shane says, and I don't.

We continue to have our quiet conversation, drinking our coffee until the woman working the cafe says, "Everyone, the cafe is closed. Please make your way back to your seats as we will be arriving in Boston soon."

We collect our trash and put it in the can, following the rest of the patrons out of the cafe car. When we get to our seats, Heath pouts.

"It's only for a few more minutes, dear," I tell him, and he nods but doesn't look happy having to go back to his seat.

I settle into my seat, and Shane once again sits down next to me, grabbing my hand to hold. I love that he is a touchy-feely guy, who is not shy with public displays of affection, and it makes me smile.

"What's that smile for?" he asks with his own smile.

"I'm just happy you don't mind PDAs," I tell him, and he laughs, kissing the back of my hand.

"Not with you, I'm not. I want everyone to know you are mine," he tells me quietly before kissing my lips softly.

I can feel the train slowing down, and I know we are pulling up to the station in Boston. Shane pulls away from the kiss, and we both sigh, not wanting to deal with work.

Once the train stops, the doors open, and people gather their belongings and begin to debark. Shane and I stay seated, waiting for Cassanova to make his appearance.

Nora boards the train and finds our car, handing Shane the search warrant.

"So why did I have to bug a judge this early in the morning for access to the private cars?" she asks.

Shane explains Cassanova to her and the fact that we have not seen him since the cafe opened.

"So, you think he could be hiding out in one of the private quarters?"

"It's probable since there is nowhere else for him to be," I say.

"Well, let's go search for our suspect then," she says, and we all stand up.

Another conductor comes through the car, and I stop him.

"Excuse me, could you tell us where the private cars are located?" I ask.

"Do you have a ticket?" he asks, looking me up and down.

"No, we," I say, pointing to the group of us, "Have a badge and search warrant, and we want to see your private cars."

"I'm sorry," he stammers. "Right this way, officers."

"Agents," Heath and I say at the same time Nora and Shane say, "Detectives."

He turns looking at us, and I'm sure it was confusing for him because then, he says, "Can I see some IDs."

Heath and I show him our FBI Badges while Shane and Nora show him their badges.

"Shit," he mutters. "Right this way."

He leads us past the cafe through a door I never noticed. It's a long hallway, and there are several closed doors to the left side.

Shane tries one of the room doors, and it's locked.

"Open it," he tells the conductor, and the man tries to argue.

"We can't do that. It goes against our patron's privacy."

"My search warrant says I have every right," Shane tells him.

The man's face blanches, and he unlocks the door. Ironically, the room is empty.

"If the room is empty, why was the door locked?" Nora asks, and the man's face grows paler.

"That room...is...sometimes used...by the staff," he stammers out.

"We are looking for Cavanaugh, AKA Casanova, where is he?" I ask, no longer in the mood for games.

"Down there," he whispers.

"Let's go," I say, following behind the conductor.

We walk down three more doors, I can hear noises coming from the room that the conductor stops at.

"No fucking way," Heath says.

"Open it," I tell him.

"But," the man starts, and I give him a look.

"Open it," I grit out, not in the mood to be nice anymore.

He unlocks the door, and I slam it open.

"What the fuck?" Cavanaugh screeches out as he tries to jump up off the bed. The female he is currently in bed with screams and tries to cover herself up.

"Sorry to ruin your fun, Cassanova, however we have some questions for you," I tell him.

"Bitch, I gave you your opportunity, now you are going to have to wait your turn. Plus, you have too many people," he says.

Shane gets to him before I can say anything and grabs him by the neck.

"I told you last time, don't make me say it again. Handcuff him," he says, throwing Cavanaugh towards the door.

"What the hell? You're cops?"

"No, they are Detectives with Boston homicide, we," I say, pointing to myself and Heath, "Are FBI agents, and you are wanted for questioning."

"Can't I get dressed first?" he asks.

"Don't you want everyone to see Casanova's goods?" I ask, looking serious.

"Do you like what you see?" he asks.

Without thinking, both Heath and I say, "What's to see?"

"Honey, you could have at least been honest with the man, instead of faking it," Heath tells the woman seriously, and I have to stifle a laugh.

She looks completely appalled.

Shane gruffs out, "Put your pants on. I don't want a limp dick or a hairy ass on my seats."

"Eeeewww, he has a hairy ass? Man, you know they have a wax for that," Heath tells him.

I have to turn and walk away, I can't with these two. I wait out in the hall until they have Cavanaugh in his pants and handcuffs.

"Why am I being arrested?" he asks.

"You're not. You're being taken in for questioning," Shane tells him.

"Questioning for what?" Cavanaugh asks.

"Murder," Shane says, leading him down the hall, through the cafe, and off the train.

"I didn't murder anyone," he says adamantly.

"I'll go get the car," Nora says.

Chapter Twenty

SHANE

I throw Casanova wanna-be in the back of Nora's car. She and Heath take him to the station, promising to come back and get us, which is good because I need some time to cool off.

"You okay?" Mya asks.

"Yeah, I just need a minute to get myself together. I really wanted to hurt that guy," I admit.

"I know, but I'm glad you didn't," she says.

"No, I think you and Heath did a better job deflating his ego than I would have done giving him a beating," I say honestly and laugh because I can't help it. "Heath really has no filter. Did you see the look on that woman's face?" I add.

"I did, and I don't know if she was appalled at being called out for faking or because she thought he was good," Mya responds with her own laugh.

"Hopefully, he'll have some answers for us," I tell her as Nora pulls up.

I open the back door for Mya, and she slides in. I get in the front seat, and Nora drives us back to the precinct.

"I have him in interrogation," Nora says, and Heath is sitting outside the door waiting for us. "What makes you think he could be the murderer?" she asks.

"He was the conductor in that car where every one of the murders took place. He said something derogatory to each of the women that were killed before they boarded. Then he made an offhand comment that leads me to believe if he isn't the killer, then he knows something," I tell her.

"Interesting. So going to Maine was a good trip," she says off-hand-edly.

"Getting the security footage there definitely was," I answer.

We get back to the precinct, Mya and I both go to interrogation to question Cavanaugh, while Nora and Heath go into the room next door to listen.

"I can't believe you two are cops," Cavanaugh says.

Mya says nothing but sends off a text as she takes a seat.

"Why?" I ask.

"You two were all over each other in the lobby of the train station," he comments.

"So, you like watching the couples that make out?" Mya asks, "Then when they get in your line, you like to ask them for a threesome? How often does that work?"

"Never," he says, gulping loudly.

"I don't think I believe you, and here's why. You wouldn't ask that question to every make out couple if it hadn't already happened before. I'll bet the first time, the female initiated it and convinced the man she was with that's what she really wanted. So once the cafe opened, you led them both to the private car, and you all had your fun. It was so much fun, you wanted to experience it again," Mya tells him softly.

"Yeah, so," he says, shifting in the seat, uncomfortable.

"I'll bet it pissed you off seeing all those women making out with an older man, but they wouldn't give you a little taste," I say, picking up where Mya left off.

"How did you feel watching that woman have sex in the car with everyone around?" Mya asks, seemingly genuinely intrigued for his thoughts.

"She was a whore," he says, but his breathing says he was turned on by it.

"How did you know what they were doing? I mean, you left the car after the cafe opened, and you never returned, so how did you know they were having sex?" Mya asks.

"Uhh...ummm. I don't have to answer that," he yells.

"Actually, you do, otherwise I'm going to assume you were the one to kill that couple while they were having sex, as well as the other couples that were murdered in your car," I tell him.

"I could get fired," he whispers.

"You probably already are," I tell him honestly. "You were having sex with a passenger," I add.

"Shit," he whispers.

There's a knock on the door, then Heath walks in with a file, handing it to Mya before walking out.

Mya opens the file and reads it.

"So you were arrested three years ago for stalking," she says.

"That was a misunderstanding," he calls out.

"A misunderstanding? You broke into your ex-girlfriend's house, while she was having sex with her boyfriend, and you jacked off, leaving your semen on her bedroom door," she states.

"She told me I could listen to them have sex, but then she called the cops and said I was stalking her," he admits, lowering his head.

"What proof did she have that you were there?" Mya asks him, though I can see she has a finger on it already.

"She had cameras around her house," he whispers.

So where did you hide the cameras in the car?" Mya probes.

"I didn't hide any cameras in the car?" He states.

"Then how else would you know the couple was having sex? Unless you killed them?"

Damn, Mya is good.

"I didn't kill them, I swear," he says with fear in his voice.

"Then how did you know?" she asks again.

He hangs his head down and says, "There are several cameras throughout the car."

"Did you see the couples being killed?" Mya asks.

He nods his head but doesn't look up.

"Where do you keep the video footage?" I ask.

"On my laptop," he whispers.

"Where is it at?"

"It's on the train, in my locker, in our locker room," he says, as tears fall down his face.

Nora comes into the room, "Heath and I will go get it," she says, and I nod.

"Can you tell us what you saw?" I ask him.

"Not much, they wore a black hoodie, with the hood up over their head each time. It was very hard to see a face, but I can tell you it was a female," he says.

"How can you be sure of that?" I ask.

"The way she walked first off, but also because a hoodie can't hide a big rack," he says, smirking.

When Mya and I are done questioning Cavanaugh, I take him down to booking so they can process him.

"What do you think of his theory that it's a woman?" I ask Mya.

"I wondered from the beginning if it was possible. Do you think it could be Gretchen Fischer? She's still missing, isn't she?" Mya asks.

"She is," I reply before adding, "She did have access to the drugs that were used, but what would her motive for doing it be?" I ask.

"That I don't know, but if she were selling the drugs, we should see plenty of money going into her account, and she wouldn't be so far in debt. I've not seen anything to show that she's paid huge amounts on anything to bring her debt down, but my gut says she's involved somehow, otherwise why would she run?"

"Good point," I say as Heath and Nora walk into the conference room.

"His locker was a mess," Nora says.

"I can imagine," Mya mutters.

Nora hooks the laptop up to the TV screen, and Heath gets into the laptop, finding the files. He opens up the first date in question.

'FILE CORRUPTED'

"What the hell?" I ask.

Heath clicks on the next date.

'FILE CORRUPTED'

"Was there a magnet in his locker?" Mya asks.

"There was a lot of junk in his locker, but we found the laptop on the floor of the locker and grabbed it. I didn't spend too much time looking at anything," Nora says, and Heath nods.

"Damn," I say.

"Cavanaugh thinks the killer is a woman, and we were wondering if it could be Ms. Fischer. I was hoping these videos would show us something," Mya says.

"I can ask our techs if they can retrieve anything," Heath says, and Mya nods.

"Might as well, I mean, all they can say is it's all lost," Mya tells him, and Heath nods.

"I'll catch the train back to Largo. Are you going to stay here?" Heath asks.

"Yeah, our only suspect or witness, whichever he is, is here. So, I think I need to stay. We may need to ask him some more questions tomorrow," Mya says, and my heart leaps with joy at the fact that she's staying here.

"True. Nora, can you take me back to the train station?"

"Sure," she says.

"I'll catch the train back to Largo and call you when I get an update from the team," Heath tells Mya. Then adds, "Do everything I would do and then some. Bye," he says, walking out of the conference room.

I laugh as Nora follows him out. Mya looks like she's ready for the seat to swallow her up, and that makes me laugh harder.

"Oh, stop it," she says, with a smile on her lips as her face is flushed.

"Do you want to check into a hotel or stay with me?" I ask her, hoping it's the latter.

"Stay with you," she whispers.

"I hoped you would say that," I tell her. "Come on, let's get out of here. There's nothing more we can do today. Let me show you what Boston has to offer."

"Okay, I'd like that," she says, grabbing her bag and laptop. "What is Nora's friend's name? The one who went missing?"

"Courtney White, why?" I ask.

"Maybe I can try to help her in her search while I'm here," she answers.

"I think she would like that. She could use all the help she can get," I tell her, loving that she would think of Nora.

I grab the keys to another vehicle, since my car is at the house, and lead Mya out to the parking lot.

"We can go to my house to change, then I'd like to take you out to Castle Island," I tell her.

"Sounds fun." Her beaming smile tells me she's serious.

I drive us to the house, and as soon as I have her inside, I pick her up and carry her upstairs while I kiss her lips.

"First, I need you," I tell her.

"Yes, Shane," she says, breathlessly.

I lay her on the bed, wanting to take my time, not rushing. I shed my clothes, then help her take hers off.

"We have all day, and I want to take my time exploring your body," I tell her.

"I don't know if I have that kind of time, Shane. I'm ready to explode now," she tells me.

"Let me help you with that, love," I tell her while kissing down her body until my head is between her legs.

"Shane, I need you," she calls out, and I lick between her folds, causing her to cry out.

I flick her clit with my tongue, sliding a finger inside her. "Damn, love, you are so wet. Is this for me?"

"Yes, you, only you," she calls out as I add another finger and suck her clit into my mouth, then flick it with my tongue.

I can feel when her walls tighten, and then her orgasm crashes down, but I don't stop. I keep going, wanting her to come again.

I love how her body flushes, and her eyes watch me with such intense desire.

I remove my fingers, licking the juices off them before sticking my tongue into her pussy and fucking her.

"Oh my God, Shane, oh shit," she calls out while gripping the sheets.

I continue fucking her pussy with my tongue, enjoying the taste of her. I could spend all day eating her pussy and never tire, but my cock is rock hard, wanting to be inside her. I just need her to come one more time before I allow myself the pleasure of being sheathed by her.

I delve my tongue deeper, while my thumb plays with her clit. Mya is writhing from the onslaught of pleasure I am giving her.

I feel her walls tighten, and I can taste her orgasm before she explodes, and her juices flood my tongue.

"Shane," she calls out, and I continue lapping up her juices.

Once I've had my fill for the moment, I kiss up her glistening body, stopping to suck on her nipples as I line my cock at her entrance.

"Please," she says, and I thrust into her deeply.

"'Fuck," I growl out, before I pull back and then push back in, deeper than before. I stare into her eyes before I take her lips in a kiss. Rotating my hips, I go deeper as her legs go higher.

"Damn, you feel so good, Mya," I whisper to her.

"Yes, so good," she says as her hands are running down my back. I kiss her neck before I pick up the pace. Both of us are so close to coming, I can feel it.

"Oh, God, Shane, more," she calls out, and I begin to pound into her.

I can feel her legs quiver and her pussy tighten, "That's it, baby, give it to me," I tell her as I quicken my pace, needing her to come because I can't hold off much longer.

"Come for me, love," I tell her, and we both come at the same time, me pushing into her deep as streams of my cum fill her, and I see white stars.

"Mya," I call out as she screams my name.

We spend five minutes holding each other, getting our breathing back before I finally pull out of her. I lay beside her, pulling her close to me as we both close our eyes.

Chapter Twenty-One

MYA

I'm woken by the ringing of a phone, and I hear Shane grumble as he rolls over. "It's mine," he grumbles as he answers.

"Maguire."

"Where?"

"I'm on my way," he says as he hangs up.

He looks over at me and says, "Well, love, that was a nice little break, but we have a couple of bodies that were found in the Charles River, and I have to go."

"I understand. Want me to come with you?" I ask him.

"If you would like," he tells me, getting out of bed and walking to the bathroom. I hear the shower turn on, and as much as I would love to spend the day in bed, I don't want to do it by myself, so I get up and join him in the shower.

We both make quick work of washing up, drying, and getting dressed. I quickly braid and pin my hair before sliding into my shoes, grabbing my phone, and meeting Shane downstairs, where I grab my laptop bag, and we walk out the door.

Shane drives us to the crime scene, and once we get there, I realize the location is not far from Boston General.

I follow Shane down a path flanked by trees until it opens up, and you can see the river. If not for all the police, crime techs, and police tape, this place would be absolutely stunning.

I watch Shane walk over to the officer, standing on the outside of the crime scene tape, and he speaks to him before calling me over.

"This is FBI Agent Mya Morgan, she will be accompanying me," Shane tells the officer before the tape is lifted, and we both walk under it and toward the two bodies at the river's edge. I see the coroner standing over the bodies, assessing them.

"What do we have, Max?" Shane asks, and I look around for Nora, but I don't see her yet.

"Ahh, Detective Maguire. We have a female and male, both have been dead over forty-eight hours, both have their throats slit and other than that, I'm afraid I can't tell you anything more until I conduct the autopsy."

"How were they found?" Shane asks.

"A couple of boaters found them floating out there and called it in. The dive team went and retrieved them," Max explains.

I look at the bodies, and though they are bloated from being in the water, I know them.

"Mr. Fields and Ms. Fischer," I say out loud.

"You know who they are?" Max asks.

"Yeah, they are both Directors at Boston General and have been missing for a few days," Shane tells him, rubbing his hand across his face.

"I'll get the bodies back to the morgue, confirm that these are the missing persons you think they are, and conduct the autopsies. Once I have something more, I'll let you know," Max tells us both.

"Thanks, Max," Shane says before coming to stand next to me as I look around, taking in the area.

Nora walks up, "Where have you been?" Shane asks her.

"I was following up on a lead, sorry. What do we have?" she asks.

"We may have found Mr. Fields and Ms. Fischer," Shane tells her.

"Shit," she says. "It would have been nice to confirm if they in fact stole the drugs and possibly gave them to Mr. Cavanaugh. If not him, then who?" she says, and I can't help nodding in agreement.

"I'll bet the killer thought they may talk and took care of them before they could," I say, shaking my head.

We head back up to the parking lot, as there is nothing more we can do here, and I ask Nora, "What lead do you have? Does this have to do with your friend?"

"No, not Courtney. While dropping off Heath at the train station, I thought I would talk with some of the conductors about Cavanaugh and see if they could give me any insight about him."

"And did they?" Shane asks.

"One guy, who knows him fairly well and was willing to talk to me said Cavanaugh is harmless, just a pervert. They've known each other for a few years, and he said Cavanaugh is really into voyeurism. He likes to watch couples, and that gets him off more than the sexual act itself." she tells us, but I already knew that from his files.

"Did he say anything else?" Shane asks.

"Cavanaugh did tell him about the first murder, showing him the footage. He said Cavanaugh was scared and didn't know what to do. He couldn't admit to anyone that he placed cameras in the car since that's against policy and would get him fired."

"And this guy didn't think he should say anything?" Shane asks.

"Stefan said he agreed to keep it quiet if Cavanaugh took the cameras down, and he agreed to. Stefan thought he had since he said nothing about the other murders except that bodies were discovered, though he says he shouldn't be surprised that Cavanaugh lied to him," she tells us with a sigh and shaking her head.

"We know the man is a pervert, but is he capable of murder?" I ask, musing over my thoughts.

"Maybe it's time to bring him back in for questioning," Shane says, and we all nod in agreement.

"I'll get him and bring him to the precinct," Nora says.

"Great," Shane replies.

"We are missing a whole lot of pieces in this puzzle. Why these couples? Why the train?" I mutter my thoughts out loud as I continue to muse over everything internally.

Shane and I get back in the car, we came in, and Nora gets back in hers. She heads to the jail as Shane and I drive to the precinct.

When we arrive, Commander Doyle is waiting for us. "Where's Riley?" he asks.

"She's gone over to the jail to bring the suspect back over, we have a few more questions for him," Shane tells him.

"What of the bodies that were found by the river?" he asks.

"Preliminary, we think they are Mr. Fields and Ms. Fischer, but Max will confirm and let us know more," he informs him.

"Anything else?"

"Both bodies had their throats slit, and they were dumped in the river. Max says they've been deceased over forty-eight hours, probably killed shortly after they left the hospital," Shane concludes.

"You think your suspect did it?"

"I don't think so, not based on what we know so far, but I think he knows more than what he has told us," I voice my thoughts.

"You think he knows who the killer is?"

Before I can answer, Shane's phone rings, "It's Nora," he says before answering.

"What's going on?"

"How?"

"Damn. Alright," he says, hanging up.

"Well, if he knew anything, he's not talking now," Shane says, shaking his head.

"Why?" I ask.

"Cavanaugh was found dead in his cell."

"What the hell is going on?" Commander Doyle asks.

"Seems the killer is tying up loose ends," I say.

"How could the killer get into the jail?" he asks out loud before saying, "I'm calling the Commissioner, we need to know how this happened."

He turns and heads back to his office to make the call.

"We need to find out if Cavanaugh had any visitors today," I tell Shane.

He nods and calls the jail.

I walk into the conference room and take out my laptop. I might as well do something useful while everyone is making calls.

I sign in with a VPN to the FBI's site and type in Courtney White. Nora shouldn't have to look for her friend by herself.

Courtney White, thirty-seven-year-old female, white, five-seven, blond hair, blue eyes. Looking at her picture, she is very pretty.

She worked at a software company here in Boston as a personal assistant. I know from Nora, she worked as Nora's husband's assistant. She made a pretty good salary. She has plenty of money sitting in her bank account that hasn't been touched in six months, right around the time she disappeared.

I look into her medical history and see the last time she went to see her physician was two weeks before she disappeared. I open her medical reports, and what I find shocks me.

I look up her next of kin, which happens to be her mother, Karen White. I jot down the address, knowing I need to have this conversation in person.

I walk out of the conference room as Shane is getting off the phone with the jail administration.

"What did they say?" I ask.

"They said there is no record of anyone visiting Cavanaugh, and they don't have answers as to why he is dead. He was currently in a cell by himself, and looking back at the security footage, there is a few minutes where the system rebooted, and no one noticed," he says, through gritted teeth.

I know he's upset, and I wish there was something I could say, but since there is nothing to be said, instead I ask, "Can I borrow your keys to the car?"

"Why?" he asks.

"I want to go visit Courtney White's mom in person. Get a little more information from her that I can't get through the internet."

"Do you want me to come with you?" he asks.

"No, I think you have plenty here, plus, if Max calls with the formal identification, you will need to make your notifications, and

I don't want to keep you from that," I tell him softly before adding, "I shouldn't be long."

"You're right, but text me when you get there," he says, and I agree before taking the keys and leaving the precinct.

Chapter Twenty-Two

SHANE

I watch as Mya leaves, she didn't say much, but I saw the thoughts crossing her face, she found something, but she doesn't want to tell me anything yet, and that's okay. I know she will when she has something more concrete.

Five minutes later, Nora walks in, looks around and asks, "Where's Mya?"

"She left to do something, said she would be back," I tell her, not giving her too much, as I don't want to alert her to Mya looking into Courtney just yet in case whatever she is chasing turns out to be a dead end. I prefer not to give Nora false hope just yet.

My phone rings, and it's Max.

"Max, have you confirmed the identities?" I immediately ask.

"You and the Agent were right. The bodies are those of Mr. Fields and Ms. Fischer, you are free to make your notifications to the families," he says with a sigh.

"Thanks, Max," I tell him, ending the call.

"Well, it's confirmed, and now we need to notify two families," I tell her.

"Who should we notify first?" she asks.

"Mr. Fischer, since he reported her missing," I say, knowing the man is going to be devastated.

We leave the precinct and drive to the address listed in the database for the Fischer's. Nora is quiet for the drive until we pull up to a wrought iron gate with a call box. I roll the window down and press the button.

"Can I help you?" a female voice asks.

"We are here to see Mr. Arnold Fischer," I respond.

"Do you have an appointment?" she asks.

"No. I'm Detective Maguire, my partner and I would like to speak to Mr. Fischer," I tell her.

"I apologize, Detective, please drive in," she says as the gate begins to open.

I drive up the long driveway until I see the house with a circle drive that goes around a massive fountain. The front door opens, and a female is standing by the door, waiting for us.

"Detectives, Mr. Fischer is waiting for you in the study, can I get you something to drink? Coffee? Water?" she asks, leading us to the study.

"No, thank you," we both answer at the same time.

"Mr. Fischer, there are two detectives here to see you, Sir," she says, announcing us.

"Mr. Fischer, I'm Detective Shane Mcguire, and this is my partner, Detective Nora Riley," I introduce us before shaking his hand.

The man looks like he hasn't slept in days, his gray hair messy, most likely from running his hands through it constantly with worry.

"Have you found my wife?" he asks in a rush.

"Yes, Sir, and I'm sorry to inform you…" I start, and the man breaks down crying.

"No, no," he cries out as his knees hit the floor and his face in his hands.

Both Nora and I stand there, looking down at the man as he breaks down. I look over at Nora, and she has this look on her face that I can't decipher. It's not sympathy, but it's not happiness either, it just is.

She looks at me and shakes her head before turning away. I look back down at Mr. Fischer.

"Sir, let me help you up," I tell him as I grab the underside of his arm, helping him to stand and walking him over to the couch.

"Is there someone we can call for you?" I ask him as he sits down.

He shakes his head no, unable to stop the tears.

"Here is my card, on the back is the number to the morgue. Dr. McBride is who you will speak to in order to make arrangements for your wife," I tell him.

"Thank you," he whispers before asking, "How did she die?"

"She was found in the river," I tell him, not going into more detail.

He cries out, and the lady who led us in, comes in to offer her support. I give her a nod.

"Sir, if you need anything, call the number on the front. I promise we will continue working your wife's case until we have answers."

The man continues to cry as Nora and I leave the residence.

When we get in the car, I look over at her, "What was that about?" I ask.

"I don't know," she sighs. "I think since Ben was killed, I've become desensitized to people's emotions, or maybe because I have been where they are, I don't allow myself to feel their pain. Where it used to gut me, and I would want to help them feel better, now I know there is nothing anyone can do," she says.

I don't quite understand, but I get what she is saying. Losing her husband was tough on her, and then not knowing what happened to her best friend, I can see her point of view.

We make the drive over to the Fields resident, and the notification was just as devastating. Mrs. Fields almost passed out, and we had to get her calmed down. Again, Nora was standoffish, but now I understand why.

When we get back to the precinct, Mya is there talking with Commander Doyle, and I watch as he smiles at something she said.

He sees us walk in and says, "How did the notifications go?"

"About as well as can be expected," I tell him.

He nods. "Well, you should all head out, there is nothing more that can be done tonight, and I think Agent Morgan here needs to eat," he says, smiling at her.

"Thank you, Commander," she tells him softly.

"Yeah, I could eat as well," I say, then look at her, "Do you have everything?"

"Let me grab my laptop, and then we can go," she tells me.

"Nora, do you want to eat with us?" I ask her.

"No, thank you. I think I'm just going to go home and relax a bit," she responds quietly.

"Make sure you get some sleep," Commander Doyle tells her, and she nods.

Mya walks out of the conference room as Nora heads for the door.

"Is Nora okay?" she asks.

"Yeah. I just think today was a little much for her. She's going home to rest," I tell her.

"That's probably a good idea. I don't think she gets enough sleep, though it's understandable," Mya says thoughtfully.

We walk out of the precinct, and I ask her, "What are you in the mood for?"

"How about Chinese takeout? We can get it and go back to your place. There's something I need to watch, but I need to bring you up to speed on what I found out today," she tells me anxiously.

We get in the car and drive toward my house, where I know of a really good Chinese takeout.

"While you were on the phone with the jail this morning, I did a search into Courtney White. I found out that two weeks before her trip, she went to see her physician. When I pulled the report, I was shocked to find that she was pregnant."

"What? Nora never mentioned that Courtney was seeing anyone," I say, shocked by the news.

"I know, so then I wondered if Nora even knew. I took the opportunity to see Courtney's mom, hoping that she could shed some light. Speaking with Mrs. White, she told me that Courtney often complained about not having time to date with work and schooling. Apparently, Courtney was getting a business degree so she could get promoted inside the company she was working for," Mya tells me.

"She had to have been seeing someone," I say.

"Someone she didn't want to tell her mom about," Mya admits.

I pull into the Chinese parking lot and then pull my phone out. "What would you like?" I ask her.

"Spicy pepper steak and some Lo Mein," she tells me.

I dial the number and place our order.

"Okay, so what else did you find out?" I ask her as we sit in the car and wait for our order to be ready.

"After speaking with Courtney's mom, I decided to go back to the train station and see if I could find Stefan, the gentleman Nora spoke with this morning."

"Did you find him?"

"I did. He was still at the train station, helping to load a train bound for New York. I told him who I was, and he begrudgingly agreed to speak with me. I bought him a coffee, and we sat down for a chat. I wanted to gauge his answers for myself about his thoughts on the cameras. He was adamant that his friend was not a killer, which was to be expected. I also asked him if he knew if there was a chance that Cavanaugh didn't just keep things on his laptop. His response was, "Ask him."

"He didn't know his friend was killed," I say, keeping up with her conversation.

"Unfortunately, that was when I had to inform him of the circumstances. The man went quiet, I didn't know if he was going to cry or punch something."

"What did he end up doing? Wait, hold that thought, our food is ready," I tell her before getting out of the car and walking into the restaurant to pick up our order.

When I get back into the car, I hand her the bag to hold, and I drive us to the house.

"So, what did he do?" I ask, getting us back into the conversation.

"He got up, mumbled something about being right back, though to be honest, I didn't think he would come back."

"But he did?"

"Yeah, and with a surprise. He handed me this," she says, pulling a thumb drive from her coat pocket."

"Huh? Does he think you are into voyeurism?" I ask, completely dumbfounded.

"No. When he handed me this, he told me Cavanaugh told him should anything happen to him, this needs to go to the police, so he held onto it, agreeing. He's pretty sure that it's of the murder that Cavanaugh witnessed," she tells me with excitement gleaming in her eyes.

"Well, it looks like we are having dinner and a show tonight," I tell her, and she laughs as I pull into the driveway.

I lead us into the house, "Here, I'll take care of the food, and you set up the TV," I tell her.

I get plates and dish our food out, and when I get back to the living room, she already has the laptop and TV ready to go.

We both sit on the couch, and she hits play while we both eat.

I thought we would be seeing the first couple that was killed, however we are watching the last couple. They have one hell of a make-out session before taking things further. When the killer shows up, we both set our plates down on the coffee table and move to the edge of the couch to stare at the screen.

We watch the killer sit in the seat behind the couple, true to Cavanaugh's word, the killer is in a black hoodie, with the hood pulled up. The killer stands up and slices the female's neck in one swift move. The camera changes angles and we see the look on the killer's face.

"Oh my God, I've seen that look before," Mya exclaims.

"Come on, we have to go, now," I tell her, jumping up from the couch, grabbing the keys, and running out the door.

Chapter Twenty-Three

MYA

I run after Shane, getting into the car, as he backs it up and puts it in drive. "Damn, I should have seen this," he says.

I don't tell him that I had my suspicions, but God, I really had hoped I was wrong. There is no disputing it now.

Shane is on the phone with Commander Doyle, as he drives with the lights and sirens, requesting backup be sent.

The question is, what is she going to do? She's been hiding for so long.

Shane turns his sirens off so as not to alert her of our presence. He turns up a long driveway. It's a nice property, a small farmhouse with a barn to the side. He pulls up front, and we both get out. She walks out onto the porch as we stand at the bottom of the stairs, looking up at her.

"Shane, Mya, what are you doing here?"

"Hey Nora, we need to talk with you," Shane says.

She looks at both of us, assessing, then she says, "You know."

Shane nods, then asks, "Why?"

"Because her husband cheated on her with her best friend, his assistant. When did you learn she was pregnant with your husband's baby, Nora?"

I hear Shane's sharp breath intake.

"I knew something was off for a while, but I thought it was our work schedules. The homicide rate was up, Detectives were leaving or retiring, and I was getting called out to more scenes. He was always working late, and we were barely seeing each other," she says, tears filling her eyes.

"Courtney came over for a visit before she and Ben were supposed to travel to Maine for a conference. I had made us both some coffee and the minute I set it down in front of her, she immediately took off for the bathroom. At first, I was so happy for her, and when I asked about the father, she told me it was a guy she had been seeing for a while. She was gushing about how in love with him she was. I was excited for her," she relays.

"Then you went to Maine to surprise your husband," I say, piecing it all together now.

"I took a few days off, thought we could spend some time together, reconnect when he wasn't in his conference. I had this whole fantasy played out in my head. I would surprise him when he got off the train, but instead, I got the surprise. He had his arm around her shoulder, she was snuggled into his side, and I watched as he leaned down and KISSED HER," she screams the last part.

"They walked right by me, and neither noticed. So, I followed them to their hotel, watched all weekend as they went sightseeing, eating out, and spending time together. There was no conference, it was just a way for both of them to spend a fabulous weekend together. I even watched my husband rub her belly and give her a blinding smile. I never got that look when I was pregnant, and then when I miscarried, all he told me was, *'Maybe it's for the best, babe. We both have demanding jobs.'*

"Then what happened?" I ask quietly.

"I followed them onto the train, found them in a car by themselves, making out. I watched and waited for them to realize they weren't alone. Then I saw the divorce papers sticking out of his bag, and I lost it."

I nod for her to keep going.

"They both screamed and shouted at being caught. Courtney was crying, saying she never wanted to hurt me, but they were in love, all that blah, blah, bullshit," she says with a sarcastic laugh.

"Ben was saying he wanted to discuss everything calmly. I told him I wouldn't sign the divorce papers, and he was stupid enough to tell me, *'She's pregnant with my child, and we are getting married.'* I don't know where the knife came from, I just had it in my hand, and I lunged at him, stabbing him, over and over, asking him what about our baby. Next thing I knew, he was dead on the floor, and Courtney was screaming."

"What happened to Courtney, Nora?" Shane asks.

"Do you think I'm so cold to kill a woman who is pregnant with my husband's child, Shane?"

"No, he doesn't," I tell her. "She's here, isn't she?"

Nora says nothing, but I know if we search the property, we will find her.

"What about the other couples? Why did you kill them?" Shane asks.

"No woman should ever have to feel what I felt or go through what I went through," she says.

"How did you know?" I ask her.

"I started an ad as a P.I., and women would call me wanting to know if their husbands were cheating. I would follow them," she says with a shrug.

"How did you get the NMBA?" Shane asks.

"That was easy, I blackmailed Fields and Fischer. I knew they were stealing medication from the hospital and selling it, also they were both having an affair."

"Why did you kill them?" I ask.

"Fields wanted to meet, and when I showed up, he told me I needed to do something, otherwise he would tell my partner everything. I slit his throat and then called Fischer to meet with me, knowing she was a liability."

"Cavanaugh recognized you, didn't he?" I ask her.

"I should have never gone down to booking. After the files came back corrupted, I needed to know what else he knew. I was processing him when he figured it out. He was trying to blackmail me." She laughs, before continuing, "I got him a cup of water, lacing the rim with fentanyl, then took him to his cell. I left him in his cell with a promise I would get him out."

The Commander pulls up with several cop cars.

"Nora Riley, you're under arrest for murder," Shane says, handcuffing her hands behind her back.

She looks at me and says, "I'm not sorry."

"I know," I whisper to her.

The officers begin to search her home, but something is niggling at me about the barn. I begin to walk over there, and Shane catches up.

"What are you doing?" he asks.

"I have this feeling that I need to check the barn. I can't explain it," I tell him as I walk.

I open the barn, and at first glance, nothing seems out of the ordinary except there are no animals in here, but then I hear a noise. I walk in further, and I hear it again, like chains clinking.

I walk over to a stall and find a very pregnant Courtney chained up.

"Shane, over here," I call to him as I unlock the door. "Hi, Courtney, don't be afraid, I'm Agent Mya Morgan from the FBI. You are safe now," I tell her.

Shane calls for an ambulance to be brought to the barn.

"Shane, we need to find something to get these chains off her," I call out to him.

"On it," he says, running out of the barn.

I hear a knock on the stall wall next to Courtney. I get up and check the stall next to her and find a blond female, very dirty.

"Rayeanne Burton?" I ask and watch as the tears fall down her face. "Don't worry, sweetie, help is here, we have you, and I know your parents and grandfather are going to be so relieved," I tell her.

"Mya," I hear a groggy voice call out, and it sounds like Heath.

"Heath?" I call back.

"Yeah," he says, and I walk to the stall across from Rayeanne's.

"What the hell happened? I thought you were back in Maine?" I tell him as I go to assess him.

"I don't know. One minute Nora and I were chatting, and the next I couldn't move, not one muscle, then the bitch hit me with something. How long have I been out?" he asks.

"If you are just waking up, then hours and we need to get you checked out along with the women."

"Women?" he asks.

"Courtney White and Rayeanne Burton," I tell him.

"I have a lot to catch up on. Did you get her?"

"Yes, you do, and yes, we did. Everyone is safe now," I tell him.

Shane comes back in with bolt cutters, and we get everyone out of the chains just as the ambulance shows up. We get Courtney loaded and sent to the hospital first to make sure she and her baby are okay, then Heath and Rayeanne ride in the second one.

Shane and I drive to the hospital and interview both Courtney and Rayeanne. I call Eric and let him know to tell the Burton family Rayeanne is safe, and I will be bringing her home as soon as she is released.

The doctor's check everyone over, and they are all fine. Courtney will need to stay in the hospital so she and the baby can be evaluated, but Rayeanne and Heath are cleared to leave.

I hand Rayeanne my phone so she can call her family and let them know she is safe and coming home.

"Wow, we solved several different cases with one case," Shane says, and I laugh.

"Yes, we did, and I'm happy we did it together," I tell him.

"Me too," he says with a smile, but then the smile fades, and he says, "I will need to stay here and do the reports to submit to the D.A. office."

"I know, and I need to get Rayeanne home and do my own paperwork about this case for our jurisdiction," I tell him sadly.

"Take our car, that way I have a reason to take the train and come up. We will figure everything else out," he tells me and I nod, trying to keep the tears at bay.

"Hey, we aren't over. No way am I going to find you, just to allow us to walk away," he tells me, and it makes my heart sore. "We will figure out our next steps," he says demandingly.

I smile because I love when he gets demanding.

"I know. It doesn't mean I won't miss you, and that's why I'm sad," I tell him before I kiss his lips.

Shane passes me the keys, and I lead Heath and Rayeanne out of the hospital and to the parking lot where the car is. I drive to Shane's house to get my bag and laptop before we hit the road to Maine.

"We need to stop for food," Heath says, whining.

I laugh, "I will, you both need to eat," I tell them.

We stop at Mr. Lionel's place for sandwiches to go. "Thank you, Mr. Lionel," I tell him, and not for the sandwiches.

He smiles and winks at me knowing, and we get back on the road.

I drive straight to the Burton house, and Eric is there waiting for us. I open the back door, allowing Rayeanne to get out, and she runs into her parents' arms as they all cry together. Detective Burton wraps his arms around all of them as he mouths, thank you.

"You both did good. How is your head, Heath?"

"It still hurts a bit," he answers honestly, "But I'm glad we accidentally found her," he says, pointing to Rayeanne.

"Make sure to go see your primary physician tomorrow and get fully checked," Eric says.

"I will, boss. Any news?"

"No. I'm headed to church to say a few prayers. You both go home, reports can wait until tomorrow."

"Yes, Boss," we both say at the same time. Looking at the family that is still hugging, I smile before Heath and I get back in the car, and I drive him home before I go home.

When I walk in, I text Shane, letting him know we made it safe, and Rayeanne is home. I don't get a reply, but I'm sure he's busy. I walk into my bedroom, strip, and climb into bed. Today has been a whirlwind, and I need to sleep.

I wake up to my phone ringing. I look at the time and see it's midnight, and Shane is calling.

"Hey, babe, what's going on?"

"I know I woke you, but I wanted to hear your voice," he tells me, and I melt. "Oh, and to tell you, you should probably answer your door."

"Huh?" I ask, getting up and putting my robe on.

I walk to the door, and when I open it, the best present is standing there. "What are you doing here?" I ask him, hanging up the phone and jumping into his arms.

"I had to be with you. I didn't like how we had to part ways today."

"I didn't either, but I understand we both have our jobs," I admit to him.

He kisses me deeply, then says, "Let's go to bed, and we can work everything else out tomorrow."

"Agree," I tell him with a smile as I kiss his lips again, and he carries me to the bedroom. We spend all night making love to each other, allowing tomorrow's problems to be tomorrow.

Chapter Twenty-Four

ERIC

I walk into the church in Chatam County, needing to thank God for Rayeanne's return and to ask him to bring Kim home safely.

I sit in the pew, bowing my head, when I hear a familiar voice.

"Something I can help you with, Agent?"

I lift my head and see Father Callahan standing above me.

"Father, I thought you were in Prichard County. I've been meaning to stop by and talk with you, but things have been a little..." I fall off.

"Busy? Yes, I'm sure in your line of work, you are always busy. Mind if I sit?" he asks.

"Of course not, Father," I tell him, moving over so he can sit down.

"You know, God always hears our inner prayers as well as the outer prayers," he says, and I nod.

"Father, there is something that I've wanted to ask you. That day at the lake, when I asked you if anything happened lately that struck you odd, you started to say something, but then you said no. Is it because what you knew was done in a confessional?"

"Yes, and before you ask the question, did I know I was talking to Father Mullen when he confessed, no, I didn't. I knew whoever was confessing to sin, they were hurting. They sounded so childlike that it never occurred to me that Father Mullen was that hurt child."

"Have you gone to see him?" I ask.

"Of course. God never leaves his children, but unfortunately, the children tend to leave the father. I think Father Mullen was so lost, he tried to find his way back to the father, but the devil was fighting him too."

"I know, and I hope he gets the help he needs," I say, looking up to the altar.

"The father hears your pleas as well, Agent. He knows you are doing your best, but you need to look for the father at the beginning in order to understand his plan."

I mull over his words as he stands and says, "You are welcome to visit the church anytime, Agent."

"Thank you, Father Callahan. I appreciate you speaking with me."

"I'm sure we will see each other again, until then, Bless you, my child, peace be with you, and may God be with you in finding your answers," he says as he blesses me.

I thank God for all his blessings and promise to do better, making more time for him.

I leave Chatam and drive to the State Building. I promised Michelle I would pick her up today so she doesn't have to drive home alone.

I walk into the lobby, pressing the elevator. The doors open immediately, stepping in, I press the Basement. When the elevator doors open, I walk down the hallway to Michelle's office.

"Hey babe," I call out to her as she types on her computer.

"Hey, sorry, I'm not finished yet. Give me five more minutes, and then I want to hear about the reunion," she tells me.

I chuckle and tell her, "No rush, finish what you are doing." I sit in the chair and wait for her.

Ten minutes later, she calls out, "Finished. Sorry about that."

"It's okay, I'm ready when you are," I give her a smile, and she gives me one back, but it doesn't reach her eyes anymore.

Michelle walks over to the door, closing it a little to grab her purse from behind the door, and when she opens the door back, she screams.

I look up and am shocked.

"Kim," she shrieks. "Oh my God, Kim, what happened?" Shelly asks her best friend, who is completely battered and bruised, almost unrecognizable.

I jump up from the chair, but Kim says nothing as she collapses, passing out into Michelle's arms.

Acknowledgements

To my support group, Kerrie, Carli, Dawn, Angel, and Renea, thank you ladies so much for all your love and help with my books. Keeping me straight. These books wouldn't be what they are without all of you. Thank you from the bottom of my heart.

Mikki, thank you for all you do for me. You are truly an amazing PA and friend.

To all my ARC readers, I know I say it every time, but I seriously cannot thank you enough for all the love you show to me and my stories.

To you, the readers, thank you for reading my book. I hope you enjoyed reading this series as much as I am enjoying writing it. I ask that you take a moment and leave a review and let your friends know how much you enjoyed it.

XOXO,

Bella

Special thanks to:

Getcovers.com for the Cover Design

Horus Copyedit and Proofreading for editing

Proofreading and other Author Services by Renea for proofreading

About the author

I'm an author of steamy suspenseful romance novellas.

I have always loved the idea of happy endings, but with real life drama.

I currently live in North Carolina and have always loved the beauty of the Appalachian Mountains. Hiking is one of my favorite hobbies as it helps to clear my mind and allow my imagination to roam freely.

I'm an avid reader of all genres.

I love traveling, especially to small communities, as the people are always so nice and

welcoming, with hidden gems in their sweet little towns.

Come follow me to learn more

Facebook Reader Group - Bella's Romance Readers | Facebook

Instagram – https://www.instagram.com/author_bella_lane/

Website - https://www.bellalanebooks.com

Also by

<u>Top Grunt Services Series</u>

Protected by the Bodyguard (Scott and Brianne's story)

Falling for the Bodyguard (Brody and Cami's story)

Loving the Bodyguard (Jax and Lena's story)

Shielded by the Bodyguard (Matt and Alisa's story)

<u>Heroes of Maine Series</u>

Defending Charley (Derrick and Charlene's story)

Saving Sam (Connor and Samantha's story)

Protecting Leia (Noah and Leia's story)

Healing the Quarterback (Will and Krista's story)

Saving St. Nicolas (Mike and Riley's story)

His Curvy Surprise

<u>Behavioral Unit Maine Series</u>

Run To Murder

Train To Murder